W9-AZL-755

The
Call Girls

BOOKS BY ARTHUR KOESTLER

Novels

The Gladiators
Darkness at Noon
Arrival and Departure
Thieves in the Night
The Age of Longing
The Call Girls

Autobiography

Dialogue with Death
Scum of the Earth
Arrow in the Blue
The Invisible Writing
The God That Failed (with others)

Essays

The Yogi and the Commissar
Insight and Outlook
Promise and Fulfilment
The Trail of the Dinosaur
Reflections on Hanging
The Sleepwalkers
The Lotus and the Robot
The Act of Creation
The Ghost in the Machine
Drinkers of Infinity
The Case of the Midwife Toad
The Roots of Coincidence
Suicide of a Nation? (ed.)
Beyond Reductionism: the Alpbach Symposium (ed. with J. R. Smythies)

Theater

Twilight Bar

A Tragi-Comedy

ARTHUR KOESTLER

Random House New York

Copyright © 1973 by Arthur Koestler
All rights reserved under International and Pan-American Copyright Conventions. Published in the United States by Random House, Inc., New York. Originally published in Great Britain by Hutchinson Publishing Group, Ltd., London.

Library of Congress Cataloging in Publication Data
Koestler, Arthur, 1905–
The call girls, a tragi-comedy.
I. Title.
PZ3K8194Ca13 [PR6021.04] 823'.9'12 72-10283
ISBN 0-394-48435-5

Manufactured in the United States of America
9 8 7 6 5 4 3

In Memoriam
Messrs. Bouvard et Pécuchet

The
Call Girls

The characters in this tale are fictitious,
but the authors, publications and experiments
quoted by them are authentic.

Sunday

"He ought to sound his horn," Professor Burch remarked nervously as the bus rounded a hairpin bend and without further ado was swallowed up by a tunnel, vanishing into the belly of a petrified whale lined with jagged basalt. The tunnel was narrow, and the driver had to creep along in first gear; it looked as if the sharp ridges jutting out of the rock might scratch or break a window at any moment. The engine of the ancient bus made such a racket that the Professor's neighbor, an apple-cheeked young friar, had to wait, before replying, for the end of the tunnel. "They must be experienced chaps," he said reassuringly. "After all, they do the run from the valley up to Schneedorf three times a day."

"He should nevertheless sound his horn," Hector Burch repeated, but his words were swallowed by a waterfall thundering down the rock-face and vanishing into the precipice under the narrow bridge they were crossing. They entered a second tunnel, which seemed an even tighter fit, and much longer than the first.

The young Copertinian Brother, Tony Caspari, enjoyed the thrills of the climb immensely, although he felt less confident than he pretended to be. Neither he nor Burch knew that the villagers of Schneedorf, renowned for their juicy humor, called the three tunnels on their road "the spiky virgins," and that occasionally a mail bus did get stuck in the middle one, which at a certain point had only a couple of inches' clearance on either side. When that happened, a gang of road menders—for the road was always on the mend, either after a landslide or a cloudburst—alerted by the protracted hooting which echoed from the rocks, betook themselves to the trapped bus with its trapped passengers. They were armed with long poles—straight young fir trees stripped of bark and branches—which they inserted under the front or back axle of the bus, as the case might be, and with fierce shouts of "Ho-o-oh-ruck, ho-o-oh-ruck," using the poles as levers, incredibly managed to edge the bus away from the rock-face. It was much the same method which the natives of Easter Island had once used to erect their giant statues—and presumably also the ancient Egyptians who built the pyramids.

In winter the bus mainly brought loads of Fräuleins, bristling with skis and pointed sticks. They occasionally got a little hysterical, although it had been explained to them that the gravel and salt strewn on the icy road made it perfectly safe. The largest contingents of Fräuleins were schoolteachers and postmistresses from England and Sweden. At the start of the season, most of the oafish village lads became transformed into glamorous ski teachers in red anoraks adorned with blue badges, who, at the arrival of each busload, amiably settled among themselves who should seduce which of the more promising-looking Fräuleins. There were no rivalries or quarrels; the villagers had their ritual ways of sharing out the loot, as they had their fixed ways of exchanging wedding and funeral gifts of fixed amounts in strictly traditional but eminently practical ways.

In summer, however, the village assumed a different

identity: it became a center for scientific and cultural congresses. Instead of giggling Fräuleins, the yellow bus brought loads of elderly eggheads. The present season, which had only just started, was to feature fifteen congresses, conferences and symposia; they were all listed on a leaflet, which Professor Burch had been studying with his usual single-minded concentration before they got into the tunnels. There was to be a Congress of the Society for the Study of Diseases of the Vocal Chords; an International Congress on the Technology of Artificial Limbs; a Symposium on the Responsibilities of Scientists in a Free Society; another on the Ethics of Science and the Concept of Democracy; a seminar on the Use of Solid Fuels in Rocket-Propulsion Systems; a Congress of the European Psychiatric Association on the Origins of Violence; a Symposium of the World Organization of Psychiatrists on the Roots of Aggression; the International Society for the Quantitative Study of Social Behavior was to hold a Seminar on Self-Regulatory Mechanisms in Interpersonal Interrelationships; the Swiss Poetry Club was organizing a series of lectures on Archetypal Symbols in the Folklore of the Bernese Oberland; and there were going to be three Interdisciplinary Symposia with titles which contained the three words "Environment," "Pollution" and "Future" in three different permutations.

The young friar was also studying the leaflet. "One wonders," he remarked, "why the European Psychiatrists and the World Psychiatrists can't get together when they are discussing the same subject."

"Different schools," Burch replied gruffly. "Analytical orientation versus pharmacological orientation. They are at each other's throats."

"I remember now," Tony said eagerly. "I read how they keep excommunicating each other. What a pity."

"The methods of the Church in dealing with heretics were more deplorable," snapped Burch.

"But more effective," said Tony, smiling through innocent blue eyes.

"That's a cynical remark for a member of your order."

"But we are trained to be cynical," Tony said brightly. "Every Friday in the seminar we have to build a bonfire of our illusions."

Professor Burch pointedly reached into his briefcase and extracted therefrom the galley proofs of the latest edition of his textbook on *The Quantitative Measurement of Behavior in its Social and Genetic Aspects.* It was mandatory reading for graduate students; by the time it was published, much of it would be out of date, and he would have to start preparing the next revised edition—a frustrating and lucrative business.

The bus had by now emerged from the romantic but somewhat sinister gorge through which it had battled its way; the mountains on both sides opened up, curving away into softer slopes which irresistibly reminded poor Tony of female bosoms expanding from the cleavage. The sky, which further down had been overcast, changed into the intense, saturated blue found only at great heights. The rest of the world was drenched in varied tints of green: meadows, slopes, pine woods, grass, moss and fern. There were no cornfields, no signs of cultivation, only the pastures and the woods, displaying their different ideas of greenness.

"I hate green." Dr. Harriet Epsom, who occupied the seat in front of Burch, had rotated her sturdy neck and shoulders at an angle of a hundred and thirty-five degrees to address this remark diagonally to the young friar. Her shoulders were freckled, burnt, and peeling in strips—which, Tony thought, should not happen to an ethologist, accustomed to the tropical sun. "What color do you like, then?" he asked politely.

"Blue. Precisely the blue of your eyes."

"I am sorry," Tony blurted out, blushing. Blushing was

a terrible habit, or rather, as he knew, a physiological reflex, which he could not get rid of, although he was fairly skilled in all sorts of mind-control experiments, from Yoga to autohypnosis.

"Rot. What's there to be sorry about?" snapped Harriet Epsom, or H.E. to her familiars. One of them, sitting next to her and thus in front of Tony, was a Kleinian child psychologist from Los Angeles, who wore her black hair short-cropped, and shaved the back of her neck. Tony could not keep his eyes away. He wondered whether she did it with a cut-throat razor, and was reminded of Mary Queen of Scots.

"It's just a silly habit," he said, recovering. "Did you get that sunburn in Kenya, or wherever your baboons are domiciled?"

"Rot. On the Serpentine in Hyde Park. They had a heat wave."

"What were you doing in London?"

"What do you think I was doing? Yawning my head off at a symposium on Hierarchic Order in Primate Societies. I knew what each of them would say—Lorenz and that Schaller woman, and the Russells and the rest—and they all knew what I was going to say, but I had to go. Why? Because I am an academic Call Girl. We are all Call Girls in this bus. You are still green, but you might become one in due time."

"It's the first time I have been invited to a symposium of this kind," confessed Tony. "I am madly thrilled."

"Rot. It becomes a habit, maybe an addiction. You get a long-distance telephone call from some professional busybody at some foundation or university—'sincerely hope you can fit it into your schedule—it will be a privilege to have you with us—return fare economy-class and a modest honorarium of . . .' Or maybe no honorarium at all, and in the end you are out of pocket. I am telling you, it's an addiction."

"You are pulling my leg," protested Tony.

"Maybe this show will be a little less of a circus because it is Solovief's idea, and I am a sucker for his ideas, though some say he's finished. But he always has a surprise up his sleeve—you'll see."

Dr. Epsom rotated her head back into quarter-profile, to resume conversation with her neighbor. "I have always been mad about baby-blue eyes," she remarked audibly. The young woman with the shaven neck said something in a semi-whisper, and both their backs shook with mirth.

After a final climb round two hairpin bends separated by an S curve, the bus suddenly emerged into the village. It stood on a high plateau surrounded by undulating grassland, wooded mountains, and in the distance some glaciers which were visible only on clear days. The village consisted essentially of a spacious square, formed by the white Romanesque church, the town-hall-cum-post-office, and two massive old farmhouses converted into inns. From the square, three lanes radiated in three different directions. Each started hopefully with a couple of shops and boarding houses, but after some fifty yards it petered out and became a dirt track ambling along pastures and farms. The farmhouses were square, squat and solid, built of seasoned, highly inflammable timber, surrounded by balconies with elaborate carvings, and with a bell tower to tell the men in the fields that dinner was ready, or to sound the alarm in case of fire. All over the wide open landscape, two or three farmhouses were always clustered together, but at a distance of several hundred yards from the next cluster.

"Where is the cinema?" Harriet Epsom shouted at the driver as they were crossing the church square—white, sundrenched and empty at this hour.

"The *Kino?*" the driver repeated, turning round. He had a ginger-colored, Emperor Franz Josef mustache, twirled and waxed to screwdriver points on a level with his eyes, and spoke a guttural English that sounded like Arabic. "The *Kino* is down in the valley. Schneedorf is a backward village, Miss. We have no cinema, only color television."

H.E. rotated her head towards Tony. "That stage mountaineer is trying to be funny."

"I think . . ." Tony started, but did not get further because the mustachioed driver again turned his head and announced, "Gentlemen and ladies, we are now arrived at the Kongress Building."

And there it stood, improbably, behind another sudden turn, which at the same time was the end of the road. The native building style in Schneedorf had not appreciably altered for the last three or four hundred years, yet suddenly, without warning, they were confronted with this huge, sadistic-looking, glass-and-concrete thing which some Scandinavian architect must have dreamt up in a state of acute depression.

"How do you like?" the driver asked as the bus came to a standstill.

There was silence in the bus. Then Dr. Wyndham's thin voice sounded from one of the back seats with a donnish titter: "It rather reminds one of a steel filing cabinet with plate glass in front, doesn't it?"

The remark caused some mild hilarity which dispelled the after-effects of the spiky virgins and created an atmosphere of camaraderie among the Call Girls, while they trooped up the steps to the concrete terrace in front of the austere building.

"Here comes our very own Nikolai Borisovitch Solovief," Harriet shouted as a big bear of a man in a rumpled dark suit emerged from the building and came to meet them with unhurried steps. "Our Nikolai," she added, "in full melancholy bloom."

He looks ill, Wyndham thought sadly, holding out his pudgy hand. "You do look flourishing," he said with enthusiasm.

Solovief thrust his shaggy head forward and looked at

Wyndham as if he were examining a specimen under the microscope. "He is telling lies as always," he said in a deep, cracked voice.

"It is nearly two years since Stockholm, isn't it?" said Wyndham.

"You have not changed."

"I can't afford it any longer," Wyndham tittered coyly.

The Kongresshaus was the brainchild of an adventurous operator whose life and works remain shrouded in mystery. He was the son of a postman in a lonely Alpine valley destined to take over his father's job, instead of which he ran away to South America and became a millionaire. One rumor asserted that he did it by smuggling arms, another that he ran a chain of brothels where the girls wore dirndls and had to yodel at the critical moment. However, after his first coronary episode, he underwent a spiritual conversion and made his money over to the Foundation for Promoting Love among Nations. The message was to radiate all over the world from the Kongresshaus, built in the Founder's beloved native mountains; but he died before the building was completed. After his death, the trustees discovered that the Foundation's investments yielded just enough interest to pay their salaries, and that there was nothing left to promote the message. They accordingly decided that the building could be put to best use by renting it to congresses and symposia, and leaving the promoting of the message to them. Actually, the building was originally called *La Maison des Nations,* but when somebody discovered that this had been the historic name of the most reputed and lamented brothel in the rue de Chabanais in Paris, a change was made. Although the Fräuleins during the skiing season were more lucrative, the villagers took a certain pride in being hosts to several galaxies of celebrities every year. But they had no standards of comparison, and thus did not realize that this particular busload was of exceptional quality, including three Nobel laureates and several likely candidates.

Some of the participants had arrived on that Sunday afternoon by the bus; others drove up in hired cars. There were to be only twelve of them, an unusually small number for an interdisciplinary symposium, but Solovief had insisted that this was the optimal figure which still allowed for constructive discussion—much to the distress of the International Academy of Science and Ethics, which acted as sponsor.

The Academy, financed by another repentant tycoon, was run by public-relations experts who believed that the prestige of a symposium, and of the handsome volume in which its proceedings would subsequently be published, was proportionate to the number of illustrious speakers. They liked to cram forty to fifty papers into a five-day conference, which put the participants into a condition not unlike that of punch-drunk boxers, and left no time for discussions—although the discussions were the declared primary purpose of the whole enterprise. "I am afraid," the harassed chairman would say, "that the last three speakers have exceeded their allotted time, so we are running behind schedule. If we want to get some lunch before the next paper, we must postpone the discussion to the end of the afternoon session." But when the last paper of the afternoon session had at last been delivered, it was time for cocktails.

"Twelve is my limit," Solovief had declared to the Director in Charge of Programs of the Academy. "If you want a circus, you must get yourself a ringmaster."

"But you have left out some of the most obvious people in their fields."

"Are we aiming at the obvious?"

"Twelve papers in five days," the Director had mused. "That leaves eighteen to twenty hours for discussions, which have to be tape-recorded. Transcribing the tapes costs a lot of money."

"If you are not interested in discussion, there is no point in the meeting."

"Your logic is impeccable," the worried Director had said, "but I have learned from fifteen years of experience that discussions tend to degenerate into games of blind man's buff. That is why I prefer a well-organized circus, where everyone performs his act amidst polite applause."

"What is the point of it?"

"Parkinson's Law. Foundations have to spend their funds. Sponsors must find projects to sponsor. Program directors must have programs to direct. It's a *perpetuum mobile* which circulates hot air. Hot air has a tendency to expand. For one of the most brilliant atomic physicists of our time, you are astonishingly naïve."

Solovief let him go on without saying a word. His shaggy brows and the heavy bags under his eyes were in odd contrast with their incurably innocent expression. He was unable to explain to the Director—though Gerald Hoffman was not a bad sort as Foundation officials went—how he felt about this conference, the sense of desperation which impelled him to organize it, and his suspicion that it might be a harebrained project.

". . . However," Hoffman went on, "you win, as usual. Twelve you wanted, twelve it shall be, same number as the apostles. But for Christ' sake change the title. We can't call a symposium just S.O.S., full-stop. Or maybe you wanted even an exclamation mark. It's undignified, sensationalistic, unacademic, apocalyptic, we might as well call it The Last Trumpet."

"Or The Four Riders. That would convey the idea of the circus."

"For Christ' sake, be serious for a moment. How about Strategies for Survival?"

"No. It sounds like computer war games about second strikes and overkill. Call it Approaches to Survival."

"Fine. Make it Scientific Approaches."

"I don't know what 'scientific' means. Do you? Just Approaches."

"All right then. APPROACHES TO SURVIVAL." Hoffman wrote it down with a sigh of resignation and relief.

There was a pause. Hoffman noticed that Solovief's thick athletic shoulders were beginning to show a stoop. And yet women used to be mad about him—including Mrs. Hoffman, ha-ha. It was, she explained, because of that darkly rugged face which reminded her of the Don Cossacks (but what about those heavy eye-bags?) and because of that deep voice with its faint Russian accent (which, she said, reminded her of Chaliapin). Solovief squashed his cigar, messing up a whole ashtray, and rose to go. Then he changed his mind, sat down again and asked in a casual voice, "Do you think it is worthwhile?"

The Director looked at him in surprise, then made a careful study of the condition of his own cigar.

"You ought to know best," he said at last. "If anybody else had suggested assembling twelve wise guys—even the wisest guys in their fields—to work out a plan to save the world, I would have told him that he was a crackpot and to go and get lost."

Solovief played with a pencil on Hoffman's desk.

"Perhaps you would have done me a favor by saying that."

"Perhaps, but you are not a crackpot. So what's at stake? At worst you will have wasted our money and your time."

"And at best?"

"Don't ask me to exert my imagination—I haven't got one. That's your department."

And so the project had got under way.

One of the approved rituals of all congresses, conferences, symposia and seminars is the get-acquainted cocktail party on the evening before the formal proceedings start. In this case getting acquainted was hardly necessary, as most of those present knew each other from similar occasions in the past. Cocktails had been announced on the program for 6 P.M., and with a few exceptions, the participants arrived on the dot. Including wives, secretarial staff and observers representing the Academy, there were about thirty people standing around uneasily in the recreation room, balancing their glasses of sherry or Scotch, and exchanging reminiscences of the last occasion they had met. Most of them seemed to be unaware of the magnificent Alpine panorama that beckoned through the plate glass of the French windows. At this early stage, the atmosphere was rather formal. But all knew that it would predictably and almost without transition become noisy and high.

"You would think, a bunch of suburbanites just out of Sunday Chapel," Harriet Epsom remarked loudly to Tony. "It's the fault of the wives. Keep away from academic wives. They are a species apart—dowdy, poisonous and always tired. What from—I ask you?"

H.E. herself looked certainly neither dowdy nor tired. She was leaning on a heavy walking stick with a rubber end, and wore a mini-skirt of some exotic material, revealing a pair of formidable thighs, made more fascinating by the blue veins wending their way through valleys of gooseflesh.

"Look at them—worn out and wilting. What wears them out so?"

"Maybe their husbands?" Tony suggested tentatively.

"You have got a point there. But scientists fall for just this type of little martyr."

"Beware of generalizations," fluted a voice behind her. She gave a little jump. Claire Solovief, who had overheard her last remark, planted an affectionate kiss on Harriet's ruddy cheek with too much powder on it. "I am not worn out and I don't aspire to martyrdom," she declared. "How would you describe me, Tony?"

"A—ravishing Southern belle," Tony, whose gallant vocabulary was limited, blurted out and blushed.

"Silly boy." Claire was slightly taken aback, and at the same time pleased. She had just turned the corner of forty, and could still look ravishing on her fair days, but unfortunately she had become a grandmother just a fortnight before they had left Harvard. Why had she gone and married Nikolai when she was eighteen and he twice as old? And why had Clairette, their daughter, gone and married at eighteen a surgeon twice as old? It must be running in the family, she thought—all written in those little genes.

"You are a snake in the grass, sneaking up on me like that," said Harriet with unexpected amiableness; she had a soft spot for Claire.

"And now I am going to take Brother Tony away from you," Claire said. "He hasn't met most of the people yet." This in fact had been the purpose of her butting in.

"Take him and good riddance," snorted Harriet. "But I wish you could protect me from Halder."

There was, however, no known protection against Professor Otto von Halder. His wild white mane bobbing high above the madding crowd, every inch a King Lear, he was approaching them with his inimitable gait, a combination between goose-stepping and deer-stalking. One could not help glancing at his legs—moccasins, tartan stockings, hair, knobbly knees, more hair, khaki shorts, in that order. "Hallo all and everybody," he bellowed. "When men and mountains meet, great things shall be done!"

But in the meantime Claire, by an adroit maneuver, had managed to steer Tony away in the opposite direction, pretending not to have seen or heard von Halder's approach. "Well done," said Tony when they were out of range. "I felt like a steamer being towed by a nimble tug."

"I learned that technique from Daddy," said Claire. "He was in the Foreign Service, but his real job was to act as a diplomatic chucker-out at receptions when people stayed too long. . . . Anyway, you have met Halder before. He is an exhibitionist, but not as silly as he sounds, so don't be taken in by his *enfant terrible* act."

"It isn't that," said Tony. "But I have read his book on *Homo Homicidus,* and I don't agree with him."

"Nor does Nikolai. Watch out, there is Valenti, so let's head in the opposite direction. I wish Nikolai hadn't invited Valenti. There is something sinister about his Valentino looks, if you will excuse the pun. And that silk handkerchief in his breast pocket."

"Isn't he supposed to be a wizard among neurosurgeons, with a Nobel prize to his name?"

"I know. He is also the greatest Lolita-chaser alive. He gives me the creeps." She steered Tony towards short, dumpy Dr. Wyndham with his large bald head and dimples in the cheek, who was listening patiently to whatever it was that the tall girl with the shaven neck was explaining to him. "This is Brother Tony, who will represent the Almighty at the Symposium," Claire broke in. "Tony, this is Dr. Wyndham, who, as you know, will turn all our future grandchildren into geniuses. And Dr. Helen Porter, who will save them from the horrors of early toilet training."

"Every Christian mother will bless you for your endeavors," Tony said solemnly to Helen Porter. "But I didn't realize we had another lady on the Symposium—besides Dr. Epsom, I mean."

"I am not a Participant," said Dr. Porter. "Harriet just brought me along as a sort of lady's companion."

"Poor little you," said Claire. "Nikolai may relent and admit you to one of the sessions as a Discussant."

"I protest, protest, protest," said Horace Wyndham, all dimples and titters, spreading his palms. "I don't wish to be torn into little pieces by a Kleinian."

"I have always wanted to meet a Kleinian," said Tony.

"Why?"

"Because I like the idea that we all start life as paranoiacs and then change into depressives."

"That isn't much of a joke, you know," said Helen, and turned her attention pointedly to Wyndham. "You were saying a moment ago . . ."

Claire and Tony moved on. "I seem to have been snubbed," Tony said cheerfully.

"She is a bitch. But bright . . . Hallo, Professor Burch. Have you met . . . ?"

"He sat next to me in the bus," Burch said without enthusiasm.

"He has just been snubbed by that Kleinian bitch."

"I did not know that a Kleinian had been invited," said Burch. "Had I known, I would have had to reconsider my acceptance. Solovief has the most peculiar ideas."

"She hasn't been invited. She's only a kind of camp follower brought by Harriet."

"Why do you dislike Kleinians?" asked Tony. "Do you dislike them in particular or do you dislike all Freudians in general?"

"I wouldn't know the distinction," said Burch, peering sharply over his gold-rimmed half-lenses, "any more than I am interested in the disputes between Jansenites and Jesuits. I happen to be a scientist and as such concerned with observable behavior. Show me a slice of your super-ego under the microscope and I will believe in its existence."

"I don't care about the super-ego or the castration complex," said Tony, "you can have them both. But in your books you also deny the existence of the mind, don't you?"

"I can look at a piece of brain tissue under the microscope. Show me a piece of mind under the microscope and I will believe in its existence. If you cannot do that I must regard the existence of a mind, as something distinct from the brain, as a gratuitous hypothesis which has to be eliminated."

"But a brain is merely a lump of matter, and I am told that matter has been dematerialized by the physicists into little whirlpools of energy or whatnot."

"You are repeating a favorite argument of the scientifically semiliterate."

Tony changed his tack. "Take hypnosis. Does it not show the power of mind over matter?"

"Hypnosis is a variant of a scientific technique called conditioning. It demonstrates observable changes in behavior, due to the conditioning of the subject's responses."

"But I have seen a hypnotist make warts on an old woman's face disappear in a week. Do you call a wart a behavior?"

"I certainly don't call a wart a behavior, and I have no time for mumbo-jumbo. Can you cure this?" He pointed to a leathery, lentil-shaped excrescence residing on his chin.

"I am not a hypnotist. But I think the chap I mentioned could . . ."

"I told you I have no time for hocus-pocus . . ." Claire wondered how Tony, for all his cheerfulness, would take a second snub, when fortunately she saw Nikolai approaching—his big head with the thick, graying hair lowered like a charging bull's, but in slow motion. Or was "fortunately" the right word? She knew as a fact—however indignant Professor Burch would be at such a suggestion—that Niko infallibly sensed when she needed him, whether he was at the other end of a crowded room or at a conference on the other side of the Atlantic. "You are quarreling already?" he asked, putting a fatherly hand with a hard grip on Tony's shoulder.

"Tony is trying to convert Professor Burch to Cartesian dualism."

"I would rather believe in little green men from Venus, traveling in flying teapots, than in a mind or soul which is not located in space and time and has no measurable temperature, or weight." Burch spoke with some heat. To Tony he had been condescending; in Solovief's presence he became aggressive.

"In our laboratories," Solovief said, pointing an accusing finger at Burch, "we deal with the elementary particles of matter, electrons, positrons, neutrinos and what-have-you, some of which possess no weight, nor mass, nor any precise location in space."

"We have all heard about those wonders. There has been no lack of publicity. So what do they prove?"

"They prove that materialism is *vieux jeux,* a century out of date. Only you psychologists still believe in it. It is a very funny situation. We know that the behavior of an electron is not completely determined by the laws of physics. You believe that the behavior of a human being is completely determined by the laws of physics. Electrons are unpredictable, people are predictable. And you call this psychology."

He bent his head towards Burch as if hard of hearing and anxious not to miss a word the other was saying—an attitude of Old World courtesy which had the effect of driving his opponents hopping mad. Burch did not actually hop, but nearly. He spoke in a clipped voice, "My answer is that physicists should stick to their observations and refrain from drawing specious metaphysical conclusions."

Solovief gently shook his bushy head. "Philosophy is too serious to be left to the philosophers."

"As far as I am concerned," said Burch, "you can leave it to the theologians. I am concerned with the experimental study of the conditioning of lower mammals and the applications of these techniques to our educational system. That is social engineering, based on hard facts, not on nebulous speculation."

"I am speculating," Claire broke in, "whether I should get you another sherry, or something more serious." But she was saved the trouble by Miss Carey approaching them with a tray of assorted drinks. There was something incongruous in Miss Carey carrying that tray—as if an elderly nun were handing round cocktails at a stag party. She wore her grayish hair stacked up in a bun, and the thin lips in the worn face became even thinner as she pressed them together in her concentrated effort to keep the tray under control.

"Have you met Miss Carey?" Claire exclaimed brightly. "It is really very kind of you to help with the drinks, but you shouldn't, really . . . Miss Carey," she went on to explain, "is Professor Valenti's assistant and an expert with the tapes, as you will see tomorrow. But really you shouldn't—let me . . ."

She tried to get hold of the tray, but Miss Carey pulled it away from her with an angry jerk that made some glasses spill over, and her face went white. "Don't you dare," she hissed. "It's *my* tray . . ."

Suddenly Dr. Valenti was with them, smiling, hands in pockets. "Now, now, Eleanor," he said quietly. "Has something upset you?—Miss Carey has been working too hard this last month," he explained.

But Miss Carey's anger went away as abruptly as it had arisen, she was now all smiles, a benevolent nun, her face creased with the wrinkles of innocence, offering the tray round as if it bore Christmas crackers for good children.

"And now, Miss Carey, to complete the introductions," Claire chimed in, as if nothing had happened, "you have already met my husband, and this is Professor Burch, and this is Brother Tony Caspari . . ."

"Fancy that—a man of God," Miss Carey said with a girlish giggle, and graciously moved on with her tray.

The noise had increased considerably in the course of the half hour since the get-together party had started. Two waitresses in dirndl costumes, a sulky brunette and a creamy blonde, both with unacademically sumptuous busts, had taken over from Miss Carey (who had disappeared unnoticed) and were going round with the drinks. They were permanent fixtures of the Kongresshaus, included in the rent, and it was said that Hansie and Mitzie knew more Nobel laureates, from Chemistry to Literature, than any other living women except members of the Swedish royal family. But they never dropped names, partly because they were well-behaved peasant daughters who had been taught that to gossip outside of one's own family was dangerous, and partly because the names meant nothing to them except for the culinary preferences of their bearers for *Kalbsgulasch* or *Zwiebelrostbraten.*

The dinner gong sounded and they all drifted down a perilous-looking spiral staircase of polished pine with steel handrails towards the dining room. They neither hurried nor tarried, but formed a compact troupe, rather like seminarists walking in pairs; on the staircase they had to walk singly, but at its bottom they re-formed into twosomes. The ritual saturnalia of the cocktail hour was over.

The dining room looked more like a cafeteria, with a great number of small square tables distributed chessboard fashion, each table seating four. The tables and chairs were of metal covered with gaudy plastic. There was accommodation for two hundred people, but now there were only about thirty, huddled together at adjacent tables at one end of the room.

Claire, who had to give some instructions to Hansie and Mitzie, was the last to get into the dining room. She saw that Nikolai was seated between Harriet Epsom and Helen Porter; the fourth chair at their table was empty. Although he had two women at his sides, one of them confoundedly attractive, Claire thought, he had an absent look. Helen Porter was talking with her usual intensity to Harriet, who interrupted her occasionally with a monosyllable which Claire lip-read as "rot." Nikolai was molding a piece of bread into a shrunken skull with his long, powerful fingers. He did it so expertly that one hardly noticed the black leather cap, like a thimble, which covered the stump of his missing left ring finger. She caught his eye and decided to join his table instead of playing hostess somewhere else.

"Niko's harem," Harriet uttered by way of comment as Claire sat down.

"He needs it," Claire said. "Without at least two adoring females around he feels depressed."

"What has he got to be depressed about?" Harriet said and wanted to bite her tongue off: she remembered that young Grisha Solovief had just been sent off to fight that nobody's war in nobody's land somewhere far east. Abruptly, Nikolai turned to her. "Tell me what you think, H.E. Do you think this conference is a hare-brained idea?"

"Rot. The Call Girls in their finest hour are going to save humanity. Or at least have a jolly good discussion. Or just a discussion. Or climb up a mountain." She thumped the stone floor with the heavy stick leaning against her chair. "I love climbing mountains. What did you make of that scene made by that Miss Carey?"

Solovief arranged the headhunter's trophies he had made in a neat row. There were five of them. "I did not like it much. Valenti insisted on bringing her along. She is one of his assistants."

"She looks to me more like a patient," said Helen.

Miss Carey could actually be seen sharing a table with Dr. Cesare Valenti and Professor Otto von Halder. Halder was telling a story to which she listened with demure disapproval, while Valenti wore his unwavering smile over his immaculate bow tie; both seemed to be permanent fixtures. Halder concluded the story with a leonine roar of laughter.

"When men and mountains meet," Claire remembered and giggled. "I thought he only quoted Goethe."

"What's wrong with Goethe?" Harriet protested. "He knew all about the unconscious and the split mind. *'Zwei Seelen wohnen, ach, in meiner Brust.'* Two souls inside my bosom, *ach*. Isn't that the first scientific definition of schizophrenia?"

Claire thought that Harriet's bosom could accommodate at least four souls. She couldn't stop giggling, oh dear. Helen said, "Goethe suffered from premature ejaculation and was a bedwetter."

Claire asked, as straight-faced as she could manage: "Who discovered that? A Kleinian at Yale?"

"No, at Minnesota. But that isn't much of a joke, you know."

They were off to a happy start.

Later in the evening—they had all gone to bed early, tired from the journey and the mountain air—Claire applied herself to the task of writing the first of the "long letters" she had foolishly promised to her *beau* back at Harvard.

"The Call Girls are getting more moth-eaten every year,"

she complained. "Even the younger ones look as if they had spent the night on a shelf in the public library. I wonder why they are so dull, and the more they cultivate their eccentricities, the duller. Could it be the effect of overspecialization? It is unavoidable, but it may lead to a kind of stunted personality, because they feel more and more passionate about lesser and lesser fragments of the world?" (Claire took great liberties with the use of question marks.) "And yet, even if it sounds as if I were boasting, Nikolai has got quite a remarkable team together. I only hope this galaxy won't turn into a spiral nebula, flying apart into the void?

"To continue our argument at the point we left off. You, my dear Guido, you do have an easier life. I don't mean that what you create is less important, but it does not demand this maddening, pedantic, frustrating, nerve-killing concentration on some infinitesimally small fraction of reality, sometimes for months, sometimes for years, sometimes for a lifetime? And all the glory that most of them get out of it are a few papers printed in technical journals, or maybe a book read by a few disapproving colleagues, and by nobody else. I knew it because when I had the good fortune to marry Nikolai I was one of that legion of laboratory assistants, a pretty moth in a white coat, working for my degree, highly efficient and with no future at all, except that dusty dedication and heroic drudgery as per above . . . You, on the other hand, *caro* Guido, lead an enviable existence pampered by the gods, because you can convert your frustrations into music, your ideas into paint (regardless whether good or bad), and your perplexities into poetry (regardless). Already people are beginning to buy your barbaric abstracts, and to listen to your beastly guitar, and even to read your illiterate poems? I admit that the three together are quite an achievement, so you fancy yourself a reincarnation of Renaissance Man, and despise us plodding, specialized pedants. What with your condottiere profile and the Roman swagger of your narrow hips, you are sure to make your way to the top and become the idol of all hysterical teenagers. I don't know why I feel suddenly so bitter, but when I think how Niko worries whether this or that hypothesis of his will be proven right or wrong, it seems damned unfair that your compositions cannot be proven right or wrong—except perhaps by posterity, though even the dead are subject to fashion. To acquire fame in *our* kind of work you have to be a Darwin or Einstein. But *you* don't have to be a Leonardo to become a celebrity; a few red doodles made with a loo-brush will do. Of course I don't mean *you, caro* Guido, I only want to explain why the Call Girls look so moth-eaten and why their wives are such bitches—of course I don't mean *me*.

"Goodnight for now, *caro* Guido. I am writing this on the balcony of our room, *by moonlight* if you please. (I almost started to explain that we have a full moon here, as if on your side it would be different because Boston, Mass., seems so far away)? The village is asleep, dreaming sweet incestuous dreams. There must be some calves out somewhere in a field, which I can hear but not see—each with a bell round its neck, each tinkling a monologue all for itself, to which no one listens. Exactly like having a symposium?"

Nikolai was pretending to be asleep, to give Claire the illusion of privacy. Through the open window he could see in the moonlight the intent curve of her back as she wrote her letter; he assumed that she was writing to Guido, and felt a twinge of jealousy. They had never seriously discussed Guido, nor Nikolai's or Claire's earlier episodic affairs; he had always maintained that strict monogamy was only for saints. For ordinary humans it was demonstrably a pathogenic factor whose effects all advanced societies tried to attenuate by legalized or tacit exemptions. Every culture, past and present, had tried to find a formula which would preserve the marital bond, but combine it with a certain amount of permissiveness, and none had failed so dismally as modern Christian society. The majority of the couples in Nikolai's own age group lived in a state of acute or chronic *misère en deux*. Their marriages were like parcels that had burst open in the mail-van and were precariously held together by bits of string. The Soloviefs were considered a scandalous exception. They had learned to tolerate each other's occasional peccadilloes as a kind of protection money paid to Aphrodite, the devious bitch. Nikolai was not even sure whether Claire was having an affair with Guido, or just liked listening to his guitar. But uncertainty made that mosquito bite of jealousy itch more. Reason told him he should be grateful that there was a Guido: he could perhaps fill at least a fraction of the void for Claire should Nikolai suddenly vanish from the scene. That possibility was clearly implied in the results of the last tests. But she did not know that; at least Nikolai hoped that she didn't. He had explained away that growing tiredness, which could not be hidden, as the unusually persistent aftereffect of a severe bout of the flu. If she did not believe him, she did not show it.

He turned over and slid his hand between pillow and sheet. Both felt deliciously cool. He relished simple bodily sensations—the touch of the coarse fresh linen, the fierce burning of hot pimento down one's gullet, the smell of tar, the sound of rain, the curve of Claire's back out on the balcony. What an incurable sensualist one was—a "melancholy hedonist" Claire used to call him. And why not? Must one's obsession with the perils of mankind exclude the pleasure of being alive—of being still alive? If Cassandra had been endowed with a sunnier temperament, she might have succeeded in preventing the Trojan War. Perhaps the trouble was that the prophets of doom were also merchants of gloom, starting with those desert-parched Hebrews . . . Anyway, if Claire wrote to Guido straight in front of his nose, she couldn't be having an affair with him.

Nikolai turned the light on and made a note on the pad lying on the bedside table: "A school for Cassandras." He felt suddenly cheerful and full of energy. Claire folded her letter and came in, looking dazzled by the sudden change of illumination. "Oh dear, you won't start working now?" she said, neatly arranging her writing things in a drawer.

"You have been working until now," Nikolai said meaningfully.

"I have been writing to *caro* Guido," Claire said. "He feels very lonely, having temporarily lost a valuable member of his audience. Are you making notes for tomorrow?" She dropped her dressing gown and slipped into the other bed. As Nikolai watched her, he thought that a color-print of Claire in her chaste black pajamas would make an exciting change in the pages of *Playboy*.

"I have been thinking," he said.

"You have?"

"About feelings of gloom and warnings of doom. These two attitudes must not be confused. It is a great mistake to confuse them. A warning serves a preventive, a positive purpose. Gloom does not. A warning must be life-affirming. The geese on the Capitol were not gloomy, Cassandra was. So the geese succeeded with their warning and Cassandra did not."

"Can our Call Girls be turned into geese?"

Nikolai got out of bed and started bumbling about the room, barefooted, pursuing his monologue.

"That letter Einstein wrote to Roosevelt in 1939 was two hundred words long and changed the destiny of the world. It shows that it *can* be done. It can. I know, I know, that we shall fail; but that is better than not trying."

He was beating the huge, soft eiderdown on her bed with

his fists, more bearlike than ever in his rumpled pajamas. He stopped and looked down at her, frowning; an idea seemed to be dawning on him.

"I think I shall shack up with you," he said, transferring his huge bulk with surprising agility under the eiderdown.

"Nice," said Claire. "But you don't want to feel tired tomorrow."

"I can apologize in my opening address. 'Ladies and Gentlemen, I hope you will sympathize if I am a little worn out by the legitimate demands of my seductive wife.' "

"That will do nicely to start the discussion," Claire said soberly but with a slightly throaty voice. It was their first resumption of what Burch's textbooks called species-specific mating behavior since *caro Guido* had entered the scene, and it went very well. Perhaps it was the effect of the *Höhenluft.*

"I won't go back home," said Nikolai, meaning his own bed.

"Don't," said Claire.

After a while he said, "About that Einstein letter. He and his buddies knew what the problem was, and were searching for the solution. We cannot even define the problem. Each one of us has a different definition. And that, precisely, defines our problem."

But Claire had fallen asleep, and Nikolai nearly did too. Then the images came—Grisha wading knee-deep through a paddy-field in nobody's land, Grisha crawling on his belly through a jungle which somebody had forgotten to defoliate. He gave in and took a sleeping pill.

Most of the Call Girls did likewise. Most of them were middle-aged or elderly and had some trouble in readjusting their physiological clocks, thermostats, homeostats and other built-in equipment to local time, local food and the *Höhenluft*—

the heady, ozone-rich air at 5,000 feet above sea level. Only Gustav, the weedy, ginger-haired character with the waxed mustaches, who had driven the special bus with the Call Girls, was still awake, listening to the radio in the basement of the vast filing cabinet. He was the janitor, handyman and P.R.O. of the Kongresshaus. His boots on the table, he was listening to the American Forces Program to improve his English. Then he turned on the midnight news, for he knew that in the morning several participants, in the absence of foreign newspapers, would ask him jokingly whether the big war had started yet. As a matter of fact it sounded as if it might at any minute.

One of the reasons for Solovief's chronic feelings of guilt was the fact that he had never know poverty. His father, a St. Petersburg banker, had foreseen the shape of things to come and emigrated with his family to Geneva just in time before the outbreak of the First World War. Niko was born on the day war was declared, but his parents did not consider this a bad omen.

Nor did they have any reason to do so. At ten, he was regarded as a musical prodigy. At fifteen, he gave his first public piano concert, favorably reviewed in the *Journal de Genève*. But success did not go to his head. Nor the adulation of his two sisters and their adolescent girl friends, which he endured with a certain gruff grace. He was a boy of dark good looks, given to sudden outbursts of temper which vanished without aftermath, rather childish for his age in some respects, precociously mature in others. The gawkiness in moving his huge frame about was in striking contrast to the nimble ease of his fingers working on the keyboard, as if to illustrate the mysterious control of mind over body. His apparent shyness was more a matter of good manners, which discreetly sheltered a considerable amount of self-assurance. At school his performance was mediocre, except in the classics, and he particularly detested physics and chemistry, both taught by elderly, somnolent masters.

A few months after the concert, he had a revelation which was to be decisive for his future. He was reading in his bedroom a history of Greek civilization. He was intrigued by the semilegendary figure of Pythagoras—the only man, according to tradition, who could perceive, with mortal ears, the music of the spheres made by the planets' motions in their orbits. Their swift revolutions caused a musical hum throughout the universe; and since each planet moved round the earth at a different speed, each hummed or sang at a different pitch. The musical interval between Earth and Moon was that of a tone; Moon to Mercury a semitone, Mercury to Venus a semitone, Venus to Sun a minor third, Sun to Mars a tone, and so on. The resulting musical scale—the Pythagorean scale—defined "the harmony of the spheres." Ordinary mortals cannot hear it, because they are made of all too solid flesh; but to Pythagoras, who was half divine, the universe was a musical box playing its nocturnes through all eternity.

Nikolai had a feeling of *déjà vu:* a passage in *A Mid-Summer Night's Dream,* recently read at school, came floating into his mind:

"Soft stillness and the night . . . Look how the floor of heaven/is thick inlaid with patines of bright gold;/there's not the smallest orb which thou beholdst/but in his motion like an angel sings . . ."

Later on he was to discover that the Pythagorean fantasy of musical harmonies governing the motions of the stars had never lost its hold on mankind. Its echoes could be found in the poets of Elizabethan England; in Milton's "Heavenly tune which none can hear/Of human mould with gross unpurged ear"; and eventually it produced one of the most astonishing feats in the history of human thought: Johannes Kepler, mathematician and mystic, built the foundations of modern astronomy on similar speculations about the affinities between planetary motions and musical scales.

Nikolai experienced the same kind of floating, entranced feeling which he knew from rare moments at the piano when one's identity became extinguished, dissolved like a drop in the ocean. He had discovered that music, the most intimate of one's experiences, was married to the stars by the abstract laws of mathematics. According to Greek historians, the marriage took place when Pythagoras took a walk on his native island of Samos, and stopped in front of a blacksmith's workshop. Watching the sweat-glistening bodies at work, he suddenly realized that each iron rod, when struck by a hammer, gave out a different sound; that the pitch of each sound depended on the length of the rod; and that if two iron rods were struck simultaneously, the intimate sensual quality of the resulting chord depended on the ratio of their lengths. Octave, fifth, major and minor third, each had a different color and feel; but that feel depended entirely on simple mathematical relations. It was a crucial discovery: the first step towards the mathematization of human experience.

But was it not degrading to reduce human emotions to a play of numbers? He had always thought so; now he discovered that to the Pythagoreans and the Platonists it was not a degradation but an ennoblement. Mathematics and geometry were ethereal pursuits, concerned with pure form, proportion, pattern, not with gross matter; with disembodied ideas which lent themselves to profound insights and delightful games. The riddle of the universe was contained in the dance of numbers, reflected in the motions of the celestial bodies and in the melodies which Orpheus played on his lyre. The Pythagoreans had been worshipers of the Orphic mystery cult, but they had given it a new twist: they regarded geometrical forms and mathematical relations as the ultimate mystery, and their study as the highest form of worship, the true Orphic purge. Divinity spoke in numbers.

On that late evening in his room overlooking the Lake of Geneva, Nikolai experienced the two stages of the Orphic rite: *ekstasis* and *katharsis.* He sat down at the piano and tried to improvise a nocturne to be called *Harmonice Mundi.* After a while he realized that it was a bad imitation of Chopin. He laughed, munched a bar of his favorite Swiss chocolate and went to sleep. He did not make plans concerning the future and was unaware that it had already been decided.

He did not abandon his piano, but found less time to spare for it. His private Pantheon now contained two sets of heroes, amiably facing each other: in one row Bach, Beethoven, Mozart, Brahms, Schubert, Haydn, stopping at Schoenberg; in the other row, Archimedes, Galileo, Kepler, Newton, Planch and Einstein, Rutherford and Bohr. This second row was open-ended, and new figures were from time to time added to it: Schrödinger, Heisenberg, Dirac, Pauli. His parents were bitterly disappointed when, after passing his *baccalauréat,* he decided to study theoretical physics in Göttingen, instead of entering the Conservatoire. But they realized that it was a mature decision, and he had a way of having his way.

He now believed, with almost religious fervor, that the mystery of the universe was contained in the equations which governed the ballet of the tiny particles inside the atom, and in the Wagnerian grand opera performed by comets, stars and galaxies. Ironically, his student years in Göttingen and at the Cavendish in Cambridge fell into a period when leading physicists everywhere were abandoning that dream. A decade earlier it had indeed seemed that the universe was yielding up its ultimate secrets—that physics was close to reaching the rock bottom of reality. But the rock turned into a bottomless mud bank. Earlier on, each atom was thought to be a miniature solar system, consisting of a nucleus of protons surrounded by orbiting electrons, replicating the harmony of the spheres on a microscopic scale. The infinitely large and the infinitely small were dancing to the same tune. By the time Nikolai graduated, this beguiling vision had disintegrated into a mad Wonderland, where an electron could be in two places at once or in no place at all. All traditional, human notions of space, time and matter had gone overboard, followed by the sacred principles of logic which linked cause and effect; all certainties had vanished from the universe, to be replaced by statistical probabilities; space itself became curved, wrinkled, pockmarked with holes filled with anti-matter of negative mass; the harmony of the spheres had turned into a cacophony.

Nikolai found this situation both distressing and exhilarating. He belonged to that unorthodox minority of physicists who, like Einstein himself, refused to believe that "God plays dice with the universe." He continued to believe that the harmony was there, hidden in the cacophony—the heavenly tune which "none can hear with gross unpurged ear." His colleagues, who believed in "the world-is-a-game-of-craps" philosophy, called him an incurable romantic (his first piano teacher had used the same expression); but they could not deny his brilliance. This was the time when the so-called elementary particles of matter began to multiply like mushrooms. Originally, there had been only two: the negative electron and the positive proton. Now every year more elementary particles were discovered in the laboratories, each with weirder attributes than the last, until there were almost a hundred different kinds of building blocks of matter—neutrons, mesons, positrons, leptons, and what-have-you. The one discovered by Nikolai Solovief, which brought him the Nobel Prize while still in his thirties, was the weirdest particle of all —even weirder than the neutrino which traveled at the speed of light, had zero mass, and could penetrate the thickest armor like a bullet going through an omelette soufflée. Solovief's particle had negative mass, was repelled by gravity, traveled faster than light, and thus, according to the Relativity Theory, backward in time. Fortunately, its lifetime was so short—a fraction of a trillionth of a second—that it did not really matter. It was a ghostly particle, yet its track could be clearly seen in the bubble chamber like the condensation trail of a jet plane. Solovief called his particle the myatron, and explained in the paper announcing the discovery that it was meant as a condensation of "maya" and "metron." Both words were derived from the same Sanskrit root, *matr-,* and reflected the contrast between Eastern mysticism and Western science. The veil of Maya was the symbol of an attitude which regarded all appearances as illusions, while "metron" meant measure, the scientist's hard, quantitative approach to reality.

Niko shared both attitudes. He could never take himself, nor the myatron, quite seriously. He had predicted its existence and photographed its track, but he could not convince himself of its reality. Or rather, he could not persuade himself of the Reality of the scientist's reality. An electron which was in two places at once could not be taken seriously. The French had an expression: *"c'est pas sérieux . . ."* Niko kept repeating it, applying it to modern physics, to Adolf Hitler alias Schicklgruber, to his affairs with various girls, and above all to himself.

In 1936, he became the youngest assistant professor at the Max Planck Institute in Berlin-Dahlem, where some of the illustrious heroes of his Pantheon had worked. Now those still alive had dispersed to England and America. They could not bear the book-burnings, Jew-beatings, the feel of darkness falling from the air. Nikolai stuck it till 1938, partly because he was still hunting for the elusive myatron, partly because he was having, after many pleasant short-lived episodes, his first serious affair with a beautiful and passionate Jewish pianist. Although she could no longer appear in public concerts, she refused to emigrate because of her aged parents who lived in a small Bavarian town and would not move. During the pogroms of the celebrated *Kristallnacht,* a troop of drunken Brown Shirts in that idyllic little town dragged three orthodox Jewish elders to their barracks and had much fun in forcing them to clean the latrines with their long beards. The father of Nikolai's girl, who refused, was beaten so savagely that he died the next day. The news, and the details, reached her in a roundabout way, a week later. They were included in the farewell letter she wrote to Niko. He had a key to her flat; he found the letter on the piano and the girl in her bathtub, her wrists gaping wide open like an illustration in an anatomy book, her head submerged in the pink water, her face far from beautiful.

Before the event, Niko had regarded the regime with an aloof distaste; now its archaic horror struck him with its full, savage force. He never forgave himself for having listened to Ada's passionate outbursts against it with the poise of the detached scientist, suspecting her of exaggeration and hysteria. He left Germany a few days later, but he could not leave memory behind with the soiled linen in his flat.

The evening in Geneva when he discovered the harmony of the spheres had been the first turning point in his life; the *Kristallnacht* became the second. The third was Hiroshima.

He had been working at the Cavendish when Einstein wrote his letter to the President. When the invitation came to join the Project at Los Alamos, he accepted without hesitation, in the belief that it would expunge his guilt. It did not bother him at first that most of his colleagues did not seem to need such justification—they regarded it as an exciting exercise in a very advanced type of engineering.

He became one of the five or six chief architects of the fission bomb; his earlier work on the myatron provided some essential clues. He only realized what he had been doing when the newspaper reports on what had happened on that Japanese island came in, followed by the more detailed, classified intelligence reports.

The coveted accolade in every scientist's life came soon afterwards. It intensified his guilt. No Nobel prizes were handed out for Hiroshima; yet the theoretical discoveries for which they were given had paved the road to it.

He joined the group of influential physicists who opposed the development of thermonuclear weapons, and resigned his post just in time before being dismissed as a security risk. It enhanced his international reputation, and made him a prominent figure in the Call Girl circuit. His still-fluent Russian, the language his parents had talked at home, enabled him to find some human contacts with colleagues from the East at international conferences, but this only added to his discouragement. Most of them entrenched themselves behind the barbed wire of officialese; and when occasionally one of them opened up a little, over a bottle, reasonably safe from being overheard, Nikolai detected in his voice an echo of his own mood of despair.

What kept him going through his forties and fifties was partly Claire and the two children, partly his new field of research: the use of radioactive isotopes in the therapy of malignant diseases. He devised several improvements of existing techniques—for he could not help drawing a spark from whatever his fingers touched—but none of them represented a major breakthrough. Even so, one of the sparks he drew cost him dearly. Through a combination of faulty equipment and lack of caution, his left hand was exposed to an overdose of an experimental type of hard radiation. The left ring finger had to be removed in successive installments, and he could not be sure whether the last installment had yet been paid. A German proverb says: Give the devil a finger and he will grab the whole hand. He even suspected the devil of some psychosomatic machinations. He developed a habit of hunching up his powerful shoulders as if carrying an invisible weight. The happy self-confidence of his youth had been eroded, together with his belief in the ultimate harmony behind the veil of appearances—but the disconcertingly innocent glance had survived. Doggedly he trained himself to play the piano with nine fingers, and published a paper in a medical journal on the neuro-muscular readjustments which this involved. The paper led to some minor innovations in orthopedic surgery.

In spite of his growing depression, he paradoxically preserved his rather schoolboyish sense of humor and the faculty of enjoying the small pleasures of life—a melancholy hedonist, as Claire was so fond of saying. She had been one of his laboratory assistants, and she had from the first moment reminded him of Ada—though no one else could possibly have seen a resemblance between Ada's Assyrian type of beauty and this Southern belle chastely camouflaged in a white laboratory smock. Both had passionate temperaments—but Ada's emotions were spontaneous and sometimes hysterical, Claire's controlled, and restrained by irony.

Clairette, now happily married, took after her. Grisha was their only son. He had inherited Nikolai's innocent eyes and as much success with the girls as Nikolai had had in his time. He was to study anthropology and live with the doomed tribes of Indians on the Amazon, before the last ones succumbed to genocide. Now he was crawling on all fours in another type of jungle, fighting nobody's war in nobody's land.

Monday

At 9 A.M., on the dot, they were all seated at the long conference table of polished mountain pine, each with a writing pad and a dossier in front. The dossier was to have contained abstracts of all the papers to be delivered, but most of them, as usual, had failed to prepare them. Separated from the conference table, along the wall, sat Claire, who acted as secretary, Miss Carey, who operated the tape recorder, the Director of Programs from the Academy, Dr. Helen Porter and three other "auditors"—as such underdogs without the full status of participants were called, who had not been invited to deliver papers but were allowed to chime in during the discussions. They sat on austere upright chairs; those of the participants had arm rests. The ubiquitous mountains behind the plate-glass windows stood watch in their calm glory; one could even see the distant glaciers.

Solovief felt glad that he had insisted on a small number who could sit along a table, all face to face. With larger numbers you had to have rows of chairs and a raised lectern. The man behind the lectern would be addressing an audience, which tended to bring out the actor in him. People around a table, on the other hand, were addressing each other as individuals. It made all the difference.

Two of the chairs were empty. Vinogradov, the Soviet geneticist, had sent a telegram saying that unexpected circumstances prevented him from attending the Symposium. That obviously signified that the authorities had at the last minute refused his exit permit; the empty chairs of Soviet delegates were a permanent fixture of international symposia. The other absentee was Bruno Kaletski, last year's winner of the Nobel Prize for Peace; he had wired that he was delayed by urgent business and would arrive later in the morning. That sort of thing, too, inevitably happened among the Call Girls. Some were always late, some had to leave before the end of the conference, some came only for one day, delivered their papers, collected their fee, and dashed off again. Nikolai had insisted that for "Approaches to Survival" you either came for the whole course or not at all. As for Kaletski, it was likely that the only reason for his being late was the need to impress on the others what a busy and important person he was. He was in fact both, but also an incurable show-off, all the time ham-acting the role which he actually played in life.

Nikolai was on the point of opening the proceedings when the clock in the nearby church tower struck nine and the church bells started to toll. They were powerful old bells, the pride of the village, and as they were only a couple of hundred yards away, their majestic booming made conversation difficult. Miss Carey had put on her earphones and was recording the booms with a rapt expression. "A happy omen," Wyndham said, giggling through his dimples. "What do you say, Tony?"

"My favorite pop music," said Tony.

The bells stopped, and Solovief got up: "I declare this conference open." Head lowered, he glanced at the faces along the table with a belligerent expression. "I shall spare you the ceremonial blah-blah and proceed with my opening statement. It will take twenty minutes . . ."

He sat down heavily, lit a cigar, and began to deliver his address, elbows on the table. Claire noted with approval that he kept his shoulders squared, without the trace of a stoop, while Helen, listening with a prim expression to that resonant bass-baritone, was reminded of a remark of Harriet's: "Women don't listen to Niko's voice with their ears—it goes straight to their uterus." On two occasions during the talk von Halder, who sat at the opposite end of the table, was heard to remark "Old hat" in an audible whisper. The second time Harriet, who sat next to him, whispered back even more audibly, "Rot. He is putting it quite neatly." The others thought so too, including Halder himself, though he was prepared to die rather than admit it. In a little less than twenty minutes Solovief, speaking in an informal but precise manner, reminded them of the principal factors which made the survival of the human species an unlikely possibility, counting them one by one on his long nicotine-stained fingers.

First, the situation prevailing since the middle of the twentieth century was without precedent in history, inasmuch as prior to that date the destructive potential of man had been confined to limited areas and limited populations, whereas subsequent to that date it embraced the entire sublunary sphere, i.e. the planet itself, its surrounding atmosphere, and the totality of its flora and fauna, excepting perhaps some radiation-resistant strains of micro-organisms. Second, rapid progress in the manufacturing methods of both types of ultimate weapons, nuclear and biochemical, made their spreading inevitable and their control impracticable. The absurdity of the situation was illustrated by the fact that according to the last available statistics, the existing stockpiles in nuclear weapons equaled one Hiroshima-sized device for every one of the earth's three and a half billion people. Third, the annihilation of distance through the increasing speed of communications was in mathematical terms equivalent to a contraction of the planet's surface to an area smaller than England measured by steam-age standards. Mankind was unprepared for this situation, unable to adapt to it, and largely unaware of its consequences. Fourth, this shrinking of the planet relative to the traveling speed of missiles and men was paralleled by a simultaneous contraction of the available living space and food resources relative to population size, which was now doubling every thirty-three years and quadrupling within the lifetime of a single generation. Fifth, leading this lemming-race were the culturally backward strata of the population. Sixth, the world-wide migration from rural to urban areas resulted in the cancerous growth of cities, where more and more people were piling up in less and less space. Seven, an inevitable by-product of these runaway processes was the physical poisoning and aesthetic pollution of land, water and air, resulting in a general degradation of human existence, the corruption of values, the erosion of meaning. Eight, just as the conquest of the air and the subsequent annihilation of distance, instead of knitting the nations into a single world-community, exposed them to mutual deterrence at gun-point, so the conquest of the ether by the media of mass communication, instead of promoting understanding between nations, had the inverse effect of sharpening ideological and tribal conflicts by demagogic propaganda. Nine, in the first twenty-five years since the inauguration of the nuclear age, about forty regional and civil wars had been fought by conventional means, and on two occasions the world had been on the brink of nuclear war. There were no indications that would permit one to assume that the next twenty-five years would be less critical. Yet the danger of man's self-annihilation as a species was not confined to the next twenty-five years; it was from now onward a permanent aspect of the human condition. Ten, in view of man's emotional immaturity compared to his technological achievements, the probability of his self-induced extinction was approaching statistical certainty. The task of the conference, as he saw it, was threefold: to analyze the causes of man's predicament, to arrive at a tentative diagnosis of his present condition, and to explore the possible remedies . . .

Solovief paused and looked accusingly at his audience, as if they alone were to blame for the sorry state of the world. Then, after a glance at Claire, he continued, trying to sound casual: "That is about all—except that I would like to remind you of a certain letter Albert Einstein wrote, in August 1939, to President Franklin Delano Roosevelt. It was a short letter, abominably written, which began:

" 'Some recent work by E. Fermi and L. Szilard which has been communicated to me in manuscript leads me to expect that the element Uranium may be turned into a new and important source of energy in the immediate future . . . A single bomb of this type . . . exploded in a port . . . might very well destroy the whole port, together with the surrounding territory. . . .'

"This may well have been the most important letter in human history. I think the situation today is no less critical than it was when Einstein wrote it. The instigators of it were an Italian, Fermi; two Hungarians, Szilard and von Wiegner; and Einstein himself was German. They had formed a sort of action committee. Of course it is easier to achieve unanimity in physics than in the social sciences. I wonder nevertheless whether it is Utopian to believe that this conference might result in the formation of such a committee of action with an agreed program, determined on a direct approach to the powers that be . . . What the Einstein letter achieved might be called a miracle—a miracle in black magic. I wonder whether a miracle in white magic of a similar magnitude is beyond the reach of science . . . I realize that I shall be accused of black pessimism and rosy optimism at the same time. Let us start the discussion . . ."

There was a long silence. Then von Halder raised a hand and started talking at the same time. "Yessir," he puffed. "Very nice. But in your ten points you have forgotten to mention the most important symptoms of sickness of this contemporary society of ours, which are aggressivity, sir, and violence, *mein Herr,* and pornography, sir, and the drug mania of the youngsters, and all these tripsters and pop-outs . . . So. Therefore we must first of all . . ."

But he was prevented from explaining what to do first of all by the noisy opening of the glass-paneled French window to the terrace through which the short, dynamic figure of Professor Bruno Kaletski burst in, with a suitcase in one hand and a bulging briefcase clutched under the armpit on the other side, leaving only a few fingers free to cope with the door. Tony jumped up to come to his aid, but Kaletski held him at bay by shouting, "I can manage. I can manage," holding the door open with his knee while he ferried the suitcase through it. "Mr. Chairman," he continued in the same breath, putting the suitcase down on the floor and approaching with short, quick steps one of the empty chairs at the table, "I must apologize, but you know how it is when they suddenly want you for an emergency meeting in Washington—they are like babies crying for their nanny, and at the same time they act as if they owned you, so I apologize again, and as I see that you have already started, which you were quite right to do, I shall not expect you, Mr. Chairman, to waste time with formal greetings, but I trust you will put me in the picture with a brief résumé of the *conversazione* that I missed." While talking, his busy hands were extracting wads of papers from the briefcase and, apparently all of their own accord, arranging them in neat piles on the table. This done, the left extracted a cigarette case from a pocket, while the right shook hands with his neighbors—smiling Dr. Valenti and somnolent Sir Evelyn Blood. Then both hands cooperated in the ritual lighting of the cigarette, a kind of manual ballet, ending in a flourish which extinguished the match in midair.

"We are all very glad," Nikolai said dryly, "that you were able to make it at all. As for the résumé, my brief opening was in itself a résumé, and I am sure nobody wants to hear it a second time. You will find an abstract of it in your file."

"A vos ordres. Anything you say," Bruno remarked in a voice intended to convey what a good-natured, non-pompous person he was, while his hands, moving like a stage magician's, were getting the abstract out of the dossier. "Please proceed. I can read and listen at the same time."

"Otto was in the process of making a point," Nikolai said.

But von Halder waved an angry hand, as if chasing a fly away. "I have forgotten my point because of the interruption. Perhaps later."

He was incensed, not by the interruption—once launched, nothing could put him off his stride—but because he realized that Kaletski was determined once more to hog the discussions. It depended on the chairman. If he was weak, or too polite to assert his authority, Bruno would talk nonstop in the discussions, and keep interrupting the speakers to cross-examine them, usually starting with: "Excuse me, but I am too stupid to understand the point you are trying to make. Do you mean that . . . , or do you mean . . . , or do you mean perhaps . . . ?" and so on. And if he did know the subject, he would refer to some long-forgotten technical paper which had anticipated the speaker's point—or conversely, to some quite recent work published in some obscure journal which refuted it—and in most cases he was dead right. If he did not know the subject, he would start with, "I am of course as ignorant in this field as a newborn babe, but I have a sort of hunch that . . ." and as often as not his hunch had something to recommend it. Bruno had been a *Wunderkind* at the age of five, and was still an infant prodigy at the age of seventy-five. At five he had been admired for being intellectually so far in advance of his age; at seventy-five he was admired for being so much younger than his age. If his damned youthful zest was not firmly controlled, he would monopolize the discussions until everybody was worn down, and wreck the symposium as he had wrecked others. So it all depended on the chairman. Von Halder hoped that Nikolai had got his message—had understood his deliberately rude remark about the "interruption." He refrained from looking in Bruno's direction.

Bruno, on his part, was apparently immersed in reading the abstract that he held in his left hand, while his right was cupped behind his ear to listen to the speaker, and his thoughts ran on yet another, third track, smarting under the insult. That poor Otto with his khaki shorts and carefully disheveled white mane would obviously never grow up. He would go on playing the *enfant terrible* with rude manners and a golden boy-scout heart. To think that he, Bruno, had almost been taken in by Otto's last book, *Homo Homicidus,* when it was published a few months ago—*almost.* But then the fallacies and contradictions, camouflaged as it were by the rhetoric, were revealed one by one. He had listed them point by point—just wait for the discussion. Bruno felt like rubbing his hands, but these were otherwise occupied.

Meanwhile, Hector Burch was talking. Unlike Solovief and Halder before him, he talked standing, hands clasped behind his back. His posture reminded Horace Wyndham of what the British Army called "standing at ease" on parade, which was not the same as "standing easy"; only the latter conveyed permission to relax. Burch's voice was precise and dry, but occasionally a faint Texan drawl could be discerned like the mirage of a bubbling spring in the desert. He shared neither the Chairman's black pessimism nor his rosy optimism —"to quote Professor Solovief's own artistic way of expressing himself." Scientists should not dramatize but concern themselves with hard, tangible facts. The tangible facts were, to quote the excellent definition in a recent textbook, that "man is nothing but a complex biochemical mechanism powered by a combustion system which energises computers built into his nervous system with prodigious storage facilities for retaining encoded information." The emphasis, however, was on the word "complex." Science approached complex phenomena by analyzing the simple parts which constituted them. The simple parts underlying all human activity were the elementary units of behavior. They were reflexes or reflexlike responses to stimuli from the environment. Some of these responses were innate, but most of them were conditioned by learning and experience. The future of mankind depended on the elaboration of suitable techniques of conditioning, accompanied by suitable reinforcements. Positive and negative reinforcements—in common parlance, reward and deprivation—were mighty tools of social engineering, which allowed us to look with some confidence into the future. But just as the electrical engineer learns how to operate complex machines by learning all there is about simple machines first, so the social engineer—the behavioral scientist—studies the mechanisms of behavior in simple organisms, such as rats, pigeons and geese. Since all behavior, to quote Professor Skinner of Harvard (here Burch's voice became reverential, almost lyrical), since all behavior of the individuals of a given species, and that of all species of mammals, including man, occurs according to the same set of primary, physico-chemical laws, it follows that the differences between the activities of man, rats and geese were merely of a quantitative, not of a qualitative order; and it further followed that experimentation with organisms on the lower rungs of the evolutionary ladder provided the scientist with all the necessary elements to attain his purpose—that is, *"to describe, predict and control human behavior."* The last words Burch uttered with special emphasis, to indicate that he was again quoting revered authority . . .

"Professor Burch, may I ask you a question?" Horace Wyndham piped up with an apologetic titter. "When you talk of 'predicting and controlling behavior,' do you include the types of activity which in common parlance are referred to as, well—literature—or playing the harp?"

"Most certainly. We refer to these activities as verbal behavior and manipulative behavior, specifying in the latter case the materials or media of the manipulations involved. Both the verbalizer and the manipulator act in response to stimuli from the environment and are controlled by the contingencies of reinforcement."

"Thank you, Professor Burch," Wyndham said; and later on it was generally agreed that this had been the moment when the symposium began to divide into two camps. However, the only overt signs of the incipient split were some clearings of throats and shufflings of feet. All took it for granted that Burch—as could be expected—had made a monumental ass of himself. The majority—later on to be referred to as the Nikosians—thought what a clever bastard Solovief was to invite the most extreme, rigid and orthodox representative of a school of thought to which he was known to be passionately opposed, a school of thought which, though in slightly watered-down versions, still dominated the philosophical outlook of the scientific community. The others, however, who basically shared that outlook, but preferred to express it in less provocative and more circuitous terms than Burch, understood just as well that Nikolai had invited him as a kind of fall-guy who would reduce their position to absurdity, and resented this as a cheap trick—"positively Machiawellisch," Halder later remarked.

The uneasy pause was ended by Harriet, who had listened to Burch with an air of patient exasperation, occasionally turning her eyes to the ceiling. "Mr. Chairman," she suddenly bellowed, "I cannot see what on God's earth Professor Burch's excursion into ratology has to do with your introductory remarks about the mess we are in, and the urgency of the situation. I gather from the program that Professor Burch will read a paper about 'recent advances in operant conditioning of lower mammals' in the morning session on Thursday, so I suggest we control our impatience to hear about that subject and discuss now your proposal to form a committee of action."

"Hear, hear," Tony said half aloud, and blushed.

"You need not worry," Burch said dryly. "I believe my remarks were relevant to the points under discussion, but I do not intend to pursue them at this stage."

Dr. Valenti lifted a carefully manicured hand: "With your permission, Mr. Chairman." He was not only strikingly handsome, with his dark, insinuating eyes and faintly ironic expression, but also had a pleasantly melodious voice. "I am of the opinion, Mr. Chairman, that Professor Burch's illuminating remarks about the necessity of social engineering are of great importance to the problems outlined in your admirable opening discourse. But I would like to ask you, my dear colleagues around the table, who all share this worry about the future, whether we think that it is too Utopian to look for remedies not only in the domain of social engineering, but also perhaps in neuro-engineering—to use a term which I diffidently proposed at the last Chicago Symposium . . ."

Sir Evelyn Blood, who up to now had been lost in some gloomy daydream, seemed to come to life. "It's a horrible term which frightens the wits out of me."

Valenti smiled. "We are a horrible race, living in horrible times. Perhaps we should have the courage to think of horrible remedies."

"What exactly do you mean by 'neuro-engineering'?" Blood asked, fixing his bloodshot eyes on him.

"I shall have occasion to elaborate on it in my humble presentation at our fifth session."

Claire, sitting demurely in her upright chair, wondered whether anybody else had also noticed a strange little pantomime during that exchange. Next to her, Miss Carey sat in front of a small folding table with the tape recorder on it. When she heard Sir Evelyn's remarks to Valenti coming through her earphones, she frowned with such sudden violent anger that the plastic strap holding her earphones in place slid forward and she was just able to catch it. It made a grotesque impression, as if she were clutching a hat in a gust of wind, until at last she pushed the strap back among the wisps of gray hair, in front of the stacked bun. But already earlier on, Claire had watched with fascination the violent changes of expression in Miss Carey's thin-lipped, worn face, which she seemed unable to control. She certainly looked more like a patient than a research assistant, Claire thought.

It was Horace Wyndham's turn; his brief intervention in the discussion was wrapped in apologetic titters and giggles. He deeply sympathized, he said, with the sense of urgency in Solovief's opening remarks which, as a private individual, he fully shared, in spite of the shamefully sheltered life he was privileged to lead in the academic backwaters of Oxbridge. But however guilty he felt about this, his own field of research by its very nature could not provide any instant remedies or short-term solutions. That field of research was concerned with babes in the cradle—starting with the first week after birth—and with methods of developing their intellectual and emotive potential in unorthodox ways. He ventured to think that in a sense the sorry state of affairs in which humanity had landed itself was partly or mainly due to its splendid ignorance of these methods. The price paid for civilization was the loss of instinctual certainties as guides of behavior—with the result that civilized man was adrift like a navigator who has lost his compass and is blind to the stars. We eat too much and copulate too rarely, or perhaps the opposite is true; we impose toilet training too late or perhaps too early; mothers are overprotective or underprotective, too permissive or too prohibitory, who knows what is best for that helpless creature in its cot? We only know the results, the finished adult products, which make this society as dismal as we know it to be. His own cherished and perhaps foolish hope was that the answers to man's predicament would emerge literally from the cradle—from the particular field of research to which he had referred. There might even be signs of a possible breakthrough in the near future if certain recent experiments were to be confirmed—experiments which would be reported in his paper at a forthcoming session of the conference. But even if the results were to be positive, as he hoped, even so the beneficial effects would be slow, very slow to make themselves felt—and they could hardly be a fitting subject for an Einstein letter to Mr. President or Her Majesty the Queen . . .

Burch fought a brief battle with himself, trying to keep his mouth shut in dignified silence, and lost. Peering sharply over his lenses at Wyndham, he said: "You object to the term 'social engineering.' Is not what *you* are trying to do exactly that?"

"Oh, no. I wouldn't call that engineering. I would rather call it officiating—to the newborn." Smiling guilelessly, Wyndham looked rather like a dimpled baby himself.

There was some polite laughter, and the discussion seemed to be grinding to a halt when, with his infallible instinct for timing, Bruno Kaletski went into action.

"Mr. Chairman, with your permission . . ." He raised his left hand while his right, which had been busily taking notes all the time, continued to do so. Solovief nodded at him without enthusiasm, but Bruno went on to finish whatever he was writing with an expression of utter concentration, thus creating an expectant silence that lasted nearly twenty seconds. Then he put down his monogramed fountain pen with an air of accomplishment:

"Mr. Chairman, it seems to me that there is considerable confusion regarding the scope and aims of this conference, and the ways and means of achieving them. Speaking in my humble capacity as a social scientist—or a scientifically orientated student of society, if you prefer that label—the reason for this confusion seems to me obvious . . ." He paused, took a few quick steps to the blackboard standing against the wall, and picked up a piece of chalk. "The reason is that we are all suffering from controlled schizophrenia . . ." He wrote on the blackboard in small, neat capitals: CONTROLLED SCHIZOPHRENIA. "No personal offense—or offenses, plural—is or are meant, of course." He wrote under the previous line: NO OFFENSE. "The term is offered as a metaphor, but not purely as a metaphor. Schizophrenia, loosely speaking, means a split mind. Our minds are split . . ." With a dramatic vertical stroke of the chalk he divided the blackboard into two halves. "On the one hand, we lead, as our friend Wyndham so aptly remarked, sheltered academic lives, pursuing our scientific quests *sub specie aeternitatis*—in the sign of eternity, as it were . . ." He wrote on the left half of the blackboard: SUB SP. AET. "But pure research has no direct bearing on the ills that plague our threatened mankind. The distant galaxies we probe with our radio-telescopes won't feed the starving millions, nor bring freedom to the oppressed millions. Even applied research in the biological and social sciences is always based on long-term projects, always taking for granted that we have plenty of time before us, that the next generation will continue where we have left off and bring our modest endeavors to a fruitful conclusion. But ay, there is the rub . . ." He paused and wrote on the same line as SUB SP. AET., but on the right half of the blackboard: TOMORROW ! ? . . . "Yes, my friends, the other half of the split mind knows that there may be no tomorrow, so we feel tempted to let the galaxies look after themselves and let eternity look after itself, and concentrate all our energies, quests and endeavors on the task of ensuring that there should be a morrow. But would that not be another kind of betrayal—the abandonment of what some of us regard, if I may use that term, as our sacred mission? So we are caught between the Scylla of complacency" (he tapped hard on the left side of the blackboard) "and the Charybdis of panicky hysteria" (tap on the right side). "Some of us try, of course, in our modest ways to heal the split by devoting part of our time and energy—and if I may say so, even more time and energy than we can afford—to the commonweal, by trying to foster mutual understanding between races and nations through organizations such as UNESCO, the Peace Council, the President's Advisory Council, the Civil Liberties Board, the Conservation Society, and similar bodies to which I have the honor to belong and the privilege to contribute my modest share, either in an executive or an advisory capacity; and if I may enlarge for a moment on the practical aspects . . ."

Once launched, Bruno could no more be stopped than the engine of a motorcar whose owner had locked himself out. He went on and on, mostly about his own modest contributions (which in fact were considerable) to the work of these illustrious bodies. He had been talking for fifty-two minutes when Solovief, who had been waiting for a gap, said in a weary voice, "It's time for lunch, Bruno, if you don't mind."

Bruno glanced at his watch with a slightly dazed look and became genuinely contrite. "Sorry," he mumbled, while his hands were nimbly engaged in stuffing papers into his case, "one does get so carried away."

His momentary confusion made him look quite endearing, but they knew that at the first opportunity he would be off again.

When Sir Evelyn Blood had once been asked by a woman journalist at a literary cocktail party whether he found his surname an embarrassment and had ever thought of changing it by deed poll, he had answered with the calculated candor which he found so useful in dealing with the press: "As a poet I cannot hope that many people will read my works, but I can at least hope that they will remember my name. Do you think the names of Auden, Thomas or Eliot mean anything to the rabble? But Blood is a household word with them."

"Do you mean," the somewhat dumb lady had insisted, "that they read you because of your name?"

"Nobody *reads* me, dear lady. But every bugger in this country knows my *name*."

That was no empty boast, and rather an understatement. Although nobody ever quoted a line by Blood, for he was not the quotable sort of poet, he enjoyed an international reputation, was invited to lecture at American, Indian and Japanese universities, and no international symposium was complete without his rumpled but imposing presence. He was knighted at sixty by England's gracious Queen (who was said to have grown pale with anger when Blood asked her before the accolade whether it would hurt), and was generally considered as the Call Girl Laureate.

He had arrived late on the previous evening by hired car, which he intended to charge to his traveling expenses. He was also late for lunch. At the entrance to the dining room he paused for a moment, surveying the scene, his huge bulk nearly filling the doorframe, apparently unaware of the discreet academic stares, appraising him in his capacity as ambassador from the other culture. Then he got into motion, carrying that bulk on rather shuffling feet, but not without a certain elephantine dignity. He did not hesitate in his choice of a seat, but advanced with unwavering purposefulness, as if attracted by a magnet, to a table at which young Tony had been sitting by himself, gobbling with relish his soup, in which two fist-sized *Knödls* stood out like volcanic islands.

"I shall have to drink my soup cold," Blood said, inspecting the *Knödls.* He talked with an outrageous, plaintive, U-plus drawl; it was impossible to know whether it was meant as a parody or to be taken at face value. "Had to rush to the loo. Always before meals. It seems my bowels will only open at the immediate prospect of a refill. Most interesting, but inconvenient. Pavlovian conditioning, our idiot-savants would call it . . . You a virgin?"

Blood's shock tactics were well known, but Tony had not encountered them before. He blushed. "I have a dirty mind," he said.

"Masturbation problems?"

"That's hardly a problem any longer."

"Ambidextrous?"

Now Tony was really outraged, though he knew one should never be. He pretended to be busy with the *Knödls.*

"You misunderstood my question. It was meant metaphorically, not literally."

"I am afraid I don't follow you."

"I meant the fantasies. Hetero or homo?"

"Oh, hetero, I suppose."

"That's bad, in your position. Fornication is mortal sin. Buggery is only venial sin. As for me, I am queer as a kipper. Everybody knows it."

"I can't see kipper as a metaphor . . ."

"That's because you are lacking in poetic imagination." He laughed. Tony had expected Sir Evelyn's laughter to be, like the rest of him, of Falstaffian dimensions. It turned out to be more like a series of dry sneezes. But it fitted somehow with the smallness of the features—small mouth, small nose, small eyes in the big, round, red, fat face.

"How did you like this morning's session, Sir Evelyn?" he asked politely.

"Snoozed through most of it. That sleek dago woke me up when he talked about neuro-engineering. It stuck in my gizzard."

Mitzie, the sulky brunette, arrived with Sir Evelyn's soup and *Knödles.* He ordered a bottle of Neuchâtel. "Big bottle?" Mitzie asked. "Indeed a full bottle, *Schätzchen,*" he said, looking as if he intended to pinch playfully her bottom. Mitzie did not appreciate the *Schätzchen,* but gave Tony's glass an extra wipe with her napkin, looking into the distance. "I don't think I shall attend the afternoon session," Blood said. "There is supposed to be some wrestling competition in the village for those juicy farm boys. Like to come with me? Of course you won't. Good little boys must go to school."

"You permit me to join you?" The black-haired, raven-faced man with a French accent, who had just come in, sat down opposite Tony.

"A purely rhetorical question," said Blood. "You know that I can't refuse, Petitjacques, however much I hate your yellow guts."

Professor Raymond Petitjacques turned his raven smile on Tony. "He says 'yellow' because he thinks I am a Maoist, and he says 'guts' because he is always preoccupied with his entrails. But he is an extremely lovable man." He filled his glass with Neuchâtel.

"That's what the frogs call Cartesian lucidity," Blood said, addressing himself to Tony. *"A propos,* Petitjacques, if you want wine, you can order your own bottle."

"That would be an instance of what Veblen called the conspicuous waste of the affluent society, because I shall drink only one glass." He turned to Tony. "Do not have more of this acid beverage if you have your liver at heart, so to speak."

"A mixed metaphor cannot be excused by a lofty 'so to speak,' " drawled Blood.

"Concerning frogs," Petitjacques said to Tony, "our *cher Maître* is out of date. My compatriots have long stopped sucking delicious frog thighs soaked in garlic, and have been coerced into consuming hot dogs and hamburgers by the imperialistic coca-colonizators. *Mon cher, c'est fini.*"

"Don't you dare call our dear little Brother 'my dear,' " said Blood.

"The connotation is different. I may call even you *'mon cher'* without incurring undue risks. And as regards Cartesian lucidity you are even more out of date. Cartesian dualism has long been replaced by the Hegelian trinity of thesis-antithesis-synthesis, reflected in Marxist-Leninist dialectics. This in turn has been reinterpreted in the philosophy of Chairman Mao, but also amalgamated with the existentialism of Sartre and the structural anthropology of Lévi-Strauss. So you see . . ."

"I don't see a bloody thing," Blood said, inspecting the substantial plate of stewed meat that Mitzie had banged down in front of him. "It's goulash," he stated.

"Do you mean the dish or the philosophy?" Tony asked.

"Both."

"You are right, a goulash," Petitjacques confirmed enthusiastically. "We are cooking a very hot and piquant ideological stew. It will burn your mouth."

"Monkey chatter."

"Perhaps. But the young baboons have shown that they mean business when they invaded the citadels of so-called learning."

"And shitted all over the place. What's that to do with structural anthropology?"

"It is appropriate. You have not read Lévi-Strauss."

Blood stared at him. "You will be surprised. I had a go. Pure jabberwocky. I couldn't believe my eyes. I had another go. The dialectics of boiled, roast and smoked food—the contrast between honey and tobacco—the parallel between honey and menstrual blood—hundreds of pages of inane verbal jugglery—it's the biggest hoax since the Piltdown skull, and you lap it up—like honey."

Blood's face had gone the color of Burgundy, and his eyes were bulging.

"I didn't know that you were that much interested in anthropology," Petitjacques said. "I shall not hesitate to admit that the great man has a tendency to go off the rails. It is the Gallic tradition. But that is not the reason why the young baboons are attracted to him. It is the message he derived from his analysis of Greek mythology: 'If Society is to go on, daughters must be disloyal to their parents, and sons must destroy their fathers.' "

"And you are on the side of the baboons. An intellectual pimp."

"I am on the side of History. And History is on our side."

"I heard that rigmarole in my own baboon-days in the nineteen-thirties. But in those days the makers of History were supposed to be the so-called revolutionary proletariat. Today it's the hairy baboons."

"I am on the side of the baboons. But the situation is different. Your generation in the Pink Thirties was pathetically naïve. You rejected your own society, but you believed in Utopia—five-year plans and balalaikas. You had a double motivation: revulsion against the *status quo* and devotion to an ideal—attraction and repulsion, a negative pole and a positive pole, a magnetic field. We only believe in the negative pole. No mirages. No illusions. No programs. Just NO. *Nada, no, nix,* and down with the pigs, and *merde.*" He grinned in an amiably Mephistophelian way.

"What do you call this philosophy? Merdology? To my mind you are nothing but a clown," Blood declared.

"Who is speaking?" said Petitjacques.

"We are all phonys. But some of us are more phony than others."

Tony, who had been listening for several minutes in respectful silence, now blurted out, "You are discussing the existential vacuum as if it were a modern phenomenon. But perhaps it was always there as part of the human condition. I have just read Ecclesiastes in the new English translation. 'Vanity' has been replaced by vacuum: 'Emptiness, emptiness, says the Speaker, all is emptiness and chasing the wind.' That dates from the Bronze Age and God was still supposed to be alive then."

"Not much ecclesiastical comfort there," said Blood.

"Baal was a god of the hippies," said Petitjacques.

Blood shrugged, eyeing with suspicion the dessert which Mitzie had brought. It was a chocolate cake called a *Pischinger Torte,* a celebrated Viennese speciality out of a tin made in Ohio, of which the Foundation had bought a consignment from the American army surplus stores.

On that second night, two of the participants wept into their pillows. Bruno Kaletski wept, interrupted by convulsive hiccoughs, because he had done it again, and made himself loathsome to all with his verbal diarrhea though he had sworn never, never to do it again. And Harriet wept, her big blotchy face suddenly like a little girl's, partly out of pity for Niko, who had looked so disappointed after the disastrous opening discussion, but also because she felt too old and ugly to seduce blue-eyed Tony, for whom she had developed a violent, aching crush.

"Rot," she said aloud, and blew her nose with vigor. From the basement of the building came radio music—"The Blue Danube." That must be Gustav, the driver with the waxed mustache. He did not look unpromising—she and Helen had exchanged guesses about the quality and dimensions of his equipment. H.E. washed her face in cold water and made it up in front of the mirror. It did not look all that old and all that bad.

Five minutes later she entered Gustav's room, without knocking and without her stick, in her scarlet dressing gown. "Mind if I keep you company?" she said. "It's too hot to sleep."

Gustav was lying in his bed, sunburnt torso uncovered, smoking. He did not look the least bit surprised. He would have preferred the dark one with the shaven neck, but one couldn't always choose, and this one had her points too—haunches like a mare. "Komm here, please," he said politely, putting out first his cigarette, then the light. A moment later he remembered that scarifying experience on the Schafberg when he lay buried under an avalanche.

Claire was not weeping, though she felt rather like it. She was lying on her balcony, moonbathing, waiting for the return of Nikolai who had gone for a walk. The morning session had been a disaster, thanks to Bruno; and the afternoon one successful in the wrong way. John D. John, Jr., the young genius from the Massachusetts Institute of Technology, had given his lecture on "Computerizing the Future." With his crew-cut, regular features, earnest expression and fluent delivery in a flat monotone, he himself seemed to have been designed and programmed by one of those efficient I.B.M. computers. Claire had tried to follow him into the complexities of communications theory, of information storage and retrieval, memory banks and automated traffic, feedback and cybernetic control, character-analyzers and robot-diagnosticians, learning machines and decision-calculators, but after ten minutes she had given up, bored and repelled—although she knew that she had a right to be repelled, but not to be bored. Once you got bored with your enemy, the battle was lost. Yet how could one not become somnolent listening to the monotonous flow of words which John D. John disgorged like a string of spaghetti? She had heard it all before: that the proud mind of man was nothing but a system of linked computers, rather slow compared to hardware circuitry, but with a remarkable storage capacity of approximately 10^{12} bits of coded information, including a prodigious percentage of redundancy and noise. His biochemical combustion system was of moderate efficiency while his interrelations with the environment and in interpersonal exchanges seemed to indicate an insufficient systemization or elaboration of the feedback controls on the levels of ecological and social organization. According to the paradigms provided by current communication theory . . .

Claire had studied the faces of the Call Girls along the table. Nikolai was doodling with his lower lip pushed forward like a chimpanzee's, indicative of a mental state that she called "fogbound." Professor Burch listened with concentrated attention, occasionally nodding with approval. Von Halder had his right hand cupped behind his ear, a sure sign that he was not listening. Harriet kept handing little notes to Tony which he acknowledged with polite smiles. Blood's chair was empty. Valenti sat impassive, a handsome statue, ignoring the frequent glances cast in his direction by Miss Carey in her earphones. Wyndham's benign smile was so sustained that he seemed to be risking cramp in his dimples. Bruno was taking notes at furious speed. Helen, sitting next to Claire, was scratching under her mini.

Recalling that scene, Claire was reminded of Madame Tussaud's. But wax figures that could move about were even more frightening. Was that why people were so scared of robots—the more lifelike, the more frightening? Robots made of software, with the right elasticity, right temperature, right eye movements . . . Was that why she herself had such an irrational horror of the computer image of the mind drawn by John D. John? For, if he and Burch were right, then she herself *was* nothing but an animated figure from Madame Tussaud's, with built-in circuitry powered by chemical combustion. Whether conceived in a test tube or designed on a drawing board, matured in womb or lab, the end product would be the same: a robot called Claire. Was her revulsion against John D. John caused by the fear that he and Burch might, after all, be right? And that the drama, in which she thought she was acting, was nothing but a dance of jerking marionettes?

They now had a computer at CalTech, John D. John had explained, which could be programmed to transform the material that it was fed into Freudian or Jungian dreams, expressed in the appropriate symbols . . .

And yet the discussion after John D. John's paper had not been bad, as discussions go. None of the participants had expressed horror, or resigned acceptance, in the naïve terms of poor Claire. Those hoary metaphysical conundrums were sixth-form stuff—at least so long as everybody was sober and the tape recorder was on. But they all had restated their positions on specialized aspects of the problem with great lucidity. And though all were careful to avoid a head-on collision, the antagonism between the two camps—Nikosians and Burchers—had become more obvious and acerbated. It also occurred to Claire that Hector Burch and John D. John were her only true compatriots, Americans by birth. Nikolai, Bruno, Valenti and von Halder taught at American universities but they were Europeans, imported to her country by that reversed Gulf Stream which had transformed its intellectual climate and made it into the Mecca of science. Tony, Wyndham and Blood were British, Harriet Australian, Valenti Italian, Petit-jacques French; but somehow with all their weaknesses and vanities, they seemed more human than her two true-blooded countrymen, straight out of the Brave New World—or the waxworks.

Claire saw Nikolai approaching on the moonlit path leading to the terrace, followed by a well-defined shadow. When he joined her on the balcony he looked refreshed and cheerful.

"The woods smell of bath salts," he said. "I have been thinking."

"You have?"

"That Einstein letter. The conference will be a failure, but we must insist that it appoints a committee of action. We must bully them into it . . ."

"I am all for bullying."

"We shall have to work on them individually, in private, starting with those on our side: Harriet, Tony, Wyndham, Blood . . ."

"Blood?"

"He is a clown, and a queen—the queen of the clowns—but he *cares.* I don't understand a line of his poetry—it gives me toothache. But he is supposed to be the only poet alive who has an inkling of what quantum physics or the genetic code is about."

"Three cheers for Bloody."

"Valenti I do not like. But he will be eager to cooperate. Almost too eager, I fear."

" 'Horrible times—horrible remedies'?"

"Precisely. Then Halder. He does not like me. But he, too, *cares.* Perhaps with some diplomacy . . ."

"I am all for diplomacy."

"Bruno will talk and talk and sit on the fence. In the end he will say he cannot sign because he is a member of several official bodies. But he could be helpful behind the scenes . . . On the other side you have the two hard-core roboto-maniacs, Burch and John Junior, and that mad-hatter Petitjacques. In matters of *Weltanschauung* we have no common language. I am not even sure whether they *care.* They might regard caring as sentimental. But we had to have them to complete the spectrum and avoid giving the impression that we are biased."

"Which we are, thank God."

"Which we are. But though we hate each other's philosophical guts, emergencies create alliances. They may co-operate out of opportunism, to be on the bandwagon. Or they may not. Then at least we shall have tried, and to hell with them."

"I am all for hell. But who is going to make the diplomatic overtures to Johnny Junior or Burch? If you were to try, you might lose your patience."

"Don't worry. I have worked out a plan. On strictly conspiratorial lines. Please don't say 'I am all for conspiring.' "

"But I am."

Nikolai explained his plan. He would first talk to two or three of those closest to his ideas and they would form a sort of secret caucus, meeting every night to discuss how to steer discreetly the next day's debates, and who should try to convert whom. It sounded very conspiratorial and rather schoolboyish, but that was apparently how these things were done at international conferences. Claire was all for it, and though she did not believe for a moment that they would succeed, she felt more cheerful as they prepared for bed.

Tuesday

The second day of the symposium started peacefully enough, with Horace Wyndham's lecture accompanied by lantern slides and delivered with the apologetic smiles of a Japanese host. His paper was entitled "The Revolution in the Cradle," but, he explained, its first part should have been called The Battle of the Womb. For the womb was the most dangerous environment which man had to face in all his life, and the period spent in it was the period of highest mortality: around twenty per cent of all embryos died before they were born, not counting induced abortions.

The human embryo was generally believed to be a happy creature, but there were reasons for doubting this. Human childbirth, compared to animal, was painful and laborious, and more painful among civilized than among primitive peoples. Being born was, if the expression be permitted, a tight squeeze. Could it be that the squeeze started already in the womb? The worst danger to the unborn babe in the later stages of development was oxygen starvation, which could kill it or cause lasting brain damage. This led to the question whether relaxing the squeeze could produce the opposite effect—improved brains? Wyndham's revered friend and colleague, Dr. Heyns of Witwatersrand, had been the first to try the idea by means of a plastic decompression dome placed over the abdomen of expectant mothers . . .

"That was in the late nineteen-fifties," Wyndham went on. "You may have read what has happened since. The rate of physical and mental development among the decompressed babies turned out to be thirty per cent faster than normal, and a number of them became infant prodigies. The medical profession, which looks at new ideas as if they were something brought in by the cat, first ignored, then attacked poor Heyns. As a result, we only have a few private clinics here and there which practice his method with remarkable results for the benefit of the few who have the courage and the money to go to them, but no officially sponsored large-scale experiments have been undertaken to date . . ."

Helen Porter, from the ringside row of chairs along the wall, waved a sun-tanned, sleeveless arm at Solovief who nodded briefly.

"Mr. Chairman, surely Dr. Wyndham is aware of the objection that the high I.Q. of these super-babies is not due to the oxygen supplied to the fetus, but to the high I.Q. of their mothers . . ."

Wyndham tittered. "Tell that to the marines. I expected this point to be raised and shall go into it in the Discussion. But in the meantime let me remind you of the fate of poor Dr. Semmelweiss from Budapest, who in 1847 was the first to introduce antisepsis in the delivery ward he was in charge of. Within a few weeks, the death rate from childbed fever in that ward fell from thirteen per cent to less than one per cent. His colleagues declared that this was due to extraneous causes, called him a charlatan, and deprived him of his post. He in turn called them assassins, went raving mad and died in a strait jacket . . ."

"Spurious analogies don't prove much, you know," said Helen primly.

"I *do* know," said Horace, giggling. He then turned to alternative possibilities of revolutionizing man's fate in the cradle, or the womb. He reminded his colleagues that already in the late sixties Dr. Zamenhoff at UCLA had injected pregnant rats with certain specific hormones; the litters produced by the injected rats showed a thirty per cent increase in the weight of their cerebral cortex and had a correspondingly higher I.Q.—maze-learning capacity—than normal rats. Schenkein *et al.* had produced similar results in chicks, after injecting the eggs with a nerve-growth factor. Again, as far back as the middle sixties, McConnell, Jacobson and Unger had trained first flatworms, then rats, to respond to certain stimuli in certain ways, then extracted stuff from their brains and injected them into untrained animals. The recipients then learned the same tasks much faster than the normal controls . . .

This time it was Dr. Valenti who raised a hand, flashing golden cuff links. But Wyndham had by now acquired his own momentum, like a tennis ball bouncing down a hillside.

"I know, I know," he smiled at Valenti, "these experiments are still controversial, half the laboratories which repeated them reported positive results, the other half did not. But there is an impressive amount of evidence to show that biochemistry, within the next few years, will deliver the means to produce animals and men with vastly improved brains from the cradle onward. Though I wouldn't go as far as that illustrious Nobel laureate in Chemistry, who calmly envisaged the breeding of truly eggheaded babies brought into the world by Caesarean section to avoid the squeeze . . ." He giggled, and Blood grunted, "That, to my mind, is a joke in abominable taste."

But Wyndham reassured him: brain improvement did

not necessitate any drastic increase in size. Neanderthal men had a larger cranial cavity than *Homo sapiens,* and geniuses often had skulls of less than normal size. What mattered was richness in nerve cells and the elaborateness of their connections in the cerebral cortex, which was only about a tenth of an inch thick. However, there were less hazardous methods than those of biochemistry to produce superior brains in animals and man. In the nineteen-sixties, David Krech's team in Berkeley had demonstrated, to everybody's surprise, that teaching baby rats all sorts of playful skills made them not only livelier and brighter, but produced definite anatomical improvements in their brains. These litters were reared in a kind of rat's Disneyland, and after fifteen glorious weeks of games and lessons they were "sacrificed," as the euphemism goes. It could then be shown that their cerebral cortex was heavier and thicker, chemically more active, and endowed with a richer "circuitry" than the control litters that had been brought up in normal conditions . . .

As for man, experiments of Skeels and his team, pursued over a period of thirty years, demonstrated that one-year-old babies in slums and orphanages, who had been diagnosed as mentally subnormal, could be transformed into slightly above-average adults if they were handed over in time to foster parents who gave them optimal care and stimulation. During the first two years in their new homes, these children gained around thirty per cent I.Q. points, and no doubt their brains underwent anatomical changes similar to the Berkeley rats. A control group of twelve children, with the same background and the same diagnosis of mental subnormality, though slightly less severe, was left to their fate; all except one had to be later on institutionalized in mental hospitals . . .

"To sum up: the brain is a voracious organ. It has to be nourished from the cradle if it is to realize its full growth-potential. It appears that throughout history, most people carried brains in their heads which in the decisive early years had been starved, and thus stunted in their growth. Once this fact is fully understood, the revolution in the cradle will have started. By a crash program applying the principles already known to us, we should be able to raise the average level of human intelligence by something like twenty per cent on the I.Q. scale within a single generation. This would be the equivalent of a biological mutation, the consequences of which I prefer to leave to your imagination . . ." After a final giggle, Wyndham sat down.

Petitjacques jumped to his feet. "You want to produce *des petits vieux*. Little professors with tiny feet and big bald heads. With hypertrophic intellects and atrophic hearts. Can you not understand that our misfortune is to have too much intellect, not too little? That is the existential tragedy of man."

"How do you cure it? With LSD?" Wyndham fluted.

"Why not? Anything is beneficial if it opens the windows in your head to the wind—anything which expands the *mystique* and strangles the *logique*."

"How do you reconcile mysticism with your Marxist dialectics?"

"But perfectly. It is the synthesis of the opposites. When you partake of the magic mushroom or the sacred cactus sauce in the sacramental dialectic mood, it is a feast of spiritual gastronomy and you understand the secret of the universe, which can be expressed in a simple motto: 'Love, not Logic.' "

"Love, eh?" grunted Blood. "That's why your baboons carry bicycle chains."

Petitjacques smiled with Mephistophelean benevolence: "The medium is not always the message. The Apocalypse must precede the Kingdom. Chopping heads is more effective than chopping logic."

Nikolai rapped the table with his cigarette lighter.

"Let us take turns," he said. "Otto wished to make a remark."

Von Halder got up, and under the pretext of smoothing his white prophet's mane, ruffled it even more. "So," he said. "Professor Wyndham shows us the way to Nietzsche's superman. Perhaps. And why not? As a simple anthropologist I cannot follow Monsieur Petitjacques's philosophic flight of ideas—what do you call them? Hipsterish, tripsterish, sit-in, drop-out, pop-out or what?" He paused, waiting for the hilarity which did not materialize, then continued, "So I am not going along with Petitjacques, but I am going along with him a short way. As a simple anthropologist I know only a little about the human brain, but if the revolution promised by Wyndham is going to affect only the cortex, the seat of intelligence and cunning, and leave the areas which govern our passions unchanged—then I fear, I very much fear, that your superman will be a super-killer. Because, as I have shown and explained in my last book, man is an animal with a killer instinct, directed in the first place at his own, his very own species; he is *Homo homicidus,* who will kill for territory, kill for sex, kill for greed, kill for the pleasure of killing . . ."

"Rot," Harriet interrupted. "I am only a simple zoologist, but I know enough history to realize that all this talk about the killer instinct is just fashionable nonsense. Men don't kill out of hatred, but out of love for their gods."

"Quatsch," said Halder. "I have heard all that before."

"You have," said Harriet. "But you did not listen."

It was time for lunch.

Between lunch and the beginning of the afternoon session, the Soloviefs went for a walk.

They followed a lane which climbed gently into the pine woods, then emerged onto a vast open meadow, with a chain of widely spaced farmhouses strung out until the path vanished into the next forest round the shoulder of the mountain. Though it was July, there were patches of snow higher up on the slopes facing north.

On farmhouse after farmhouse there were handwritten notices announcing rooms to let with full board. It was the hour of the midday dinner, and Claire watched with fascination the fare being served to the families on the crowded terraces: soup with dumplings; large helpings of pork chops, cabbage and potatoes, followed by chocolate cake, washed down with beer. "I can lip-read the sounds of their munching," she said.

"Don't listen. Look at the mountains. Listen to the cowbells."

But the sound of the cowbells was blocked out by the jukeboxes and the motorbikes without silencers, which echoed like machine guns from the road lower down. The peasant boys had a craze for motorbikes—big, shiny, pepped-up brutes. They left school at fifteen, mooched about on the farm for a year or two, then half learned a trade, to become garage mechanics, electricians, plasterers or waiters, hoarding their wages until, at forty, they were able to realize their life's dream: to open another *pension* with thirty beds, offering healthy country fare out of plastic packs.

"The doctor's wife told me," said Claire, "that six years ago she ordered the first frigidaire which the village had seen. When it arrived, she explained its purpose to Hilda, the next-door farmer's daughter, who worked for her as a daily. Hilda got very excited and asked if she could borrow two ice cubes and take them down on a saucer to her husband, to put into his beer, but only for a very short while—then she would bring the cubes back. The next morning she came in with red eyes—in her excitement she had slipped on the path, broken the saucer, lost the ice cubes and spent a sleepless night. Now Hilda has a huge deep-freeze in her boarding house and all the other gadgets which the doctor's wife cannot afford. She hardly speaks to her."

"Who hardly speaks to whom?"

"Hilda to the doctor's wife, of course."

They walked on along the blissfully empty lane—the tourists were busy digesting on the terraces of the farms below, spread over flimsy deck chairs which looked like collapsing from the overload. The summer guests, unlike the winter skiers, nearly all came from those regions of Central Europe where body volume was still considered an index of prosperity. They were not beautiful to behold. The beautiful people used mountains only for skiing. In summer they wore snorkels, not rucksacks.

Nikolai and Claire made way for a family which did carry rucksacks and sticks, trudging down the lane. Claire, too, had to stand aside on the verge of the lane, confronted with the sheer bulk of the couple. Two children were gamboling as outriders in front of them. All four stared at the Soloviefs with unfathomable disapproval. When they had gone a few steps past, the woman pronounced the verdict: *"Engländer . . . !"*

Nikolai walked a little faster. Claire giggled, "That lady looked exactly like a chest of drawers mounted on stovepipes with the top drawer pulled out . . . Were they like that when you were taken on vacation as a little boy?"

"Little boys love big bosoms," said Nikolai.

"So all American men are little boys," said Claire. "I am just being silly. I know this transformation is a shock to you."

"I did love the mountains," said Nikolai. "And the mountain peasants. They called themselves not farmers but peasants —*Bauern*. They were proud of it. Official communications were addressed to 'Herrn Bauer Moser' or "Herrn Bauer

Hübner.' Bauer is still one of the commonest names in their telephone directory—but hardly anybody in ours is called John Peasant, or Jean Paysan."

"But perhaps as a little boy your view of the *Bauern* was somewhat dewy-eyed."

"Perhaps. One has no right to blame them. It was a hard life. Until they made the greatest discovery in their history: tourists are easier to milk than cows. You don't have to get up at four in the morning."

They sat down on a public bench provided by the municipality of Schneedorf, a few steps off the lane. It had a magnificent view and an advertisement for a new deodorant painted on the backrest. A few steps from them there was a souvenir stall displaying native woodcarvings of stags, mountain goats and golden eagles copied from Disney comics.

"I am not being sentimental," said Niko. "You think the tourist explosion is just a minor nuisance. But the tourist industry occupies first place in the economy of this country, and of others as remote as the Fiji Islands; and in some the annual turnover of tourists far outnumber the native population. They flood the mountains, the beaches, the islands. They turn the natives into parasites, erode their ways of life, contaminate their arts and crafts, their music . . ." Niko was getting steamed up. He hit the ground with his walking stick. "You think it's a minor nuisance, but it is a global phenomenon, spreading global corruption. It is leveling down all cultures to the lowest common denominator, to a stereotyped norm, a synthetic pseudoculture, expanding like a plastic bubble. Colonialism is dead; now we have coca-colonization, all over the world. Each nation does it to the other."

Claire knew that when he got into that mood there was no arguing with Niko. Nevertheless she tried: "Isn't there another side to it? People like that chest-of-drawers lady have never before had a chance to travel abroad. Why grudge them their fun?"

"Fun? Do you remember those busloads of blue-haired matrons on package tours in Hawaii? Two hundred of them in each package. The organizers treated them like a bunch of battery-reared hens expected to lay a golden egg per day. And they felt just like that, hating it all, the natives who robbed them, the food that gave them diarrhea, the lingo which they couldn't speak. Instead of bringing nations closer to mutual understanding, travel spreads mutual contempt."

Niko evidently had a bee in his bonnet about it. Claire could not quite understand why, although she knew that the philanthropist in him was always ready to turn into a misanthropist by the throw of a switch. Yet he always took such childish pleasure in traveling in foreign countries. Even the exotic uniforms of the customs officials delighted him.

"Have you noticed," he said, "that nothing sounds so contemptuous as a tourist calling another tourist a tourist?"

"But we both love being tourists," protested Claire.

"Ah!" said Niko. "Because we love looking out of the window of the train. But they travel like registered parcels."

Suddenly it dawned on Claire that there was some connection in Niko's mind between those dumb travelers and the Call Girls—between the tourist explosion and the knowledge explosion—and the corrosive fall-out left by both. But pursuing the subject would only get him fogbound again.

"To come back to Hilda," she said.

"What Hilda?"

"The one who used to work for the doctor's wife, and was an honest peasant woman until she discovered that tourists were easier to milk than cows. You yourself said that one cannot blame them."

"I was repeating a cliché. Blame is a word which has no place in Burch's vocabulary. Or in John D. John's. They say it is meaningless to blame a person for his deeds—or to praise him. You can judge only the chromosomes in his balls, the circuitry in his cerebral cortex, the adrenalin in his arteries, the phobias of his mum, the society in which he lives. And so on—alibis and excuses all the way, right back to Adam and Eve. They have provided even God with an alibi by declaring him dead. Remember Archimedes: 'Give me but one firm spot in the universe to stand on and I will move the earth.' We have no firm spot to stand on. In fact, no moral leg to stand on."

"But we have. You have, and Harriet has, and Wyndham and Tony. That's why we are here."

Solovief stopped to pick up a clump of grayish snow which had escaped the sun's attention in a crevice, and kneaded it between his palms into a hard ball. He aimed it at a telegraph pole and missed. "You know what I mean. To believe is easy. To disbelieve is easy. To disbelieve one's own disbelief is hard."

"I know," said Claire. "But it keeps one going."

"It keeps one going—like a squirrel in a revolving cage."

"I think we ought to get back," said Claire. "I forget who is next on the menu."

"Petitjacques." Nikolai laughed, his anger suddenly gone. "If ever there was a frenzied squirrel in a cage, it's him."

Nobody knew, even approximately, Raymond Petitjacques's age. In successive editions of the *International Who's Who* and suchlike reference books his date of birth varied up and down by as much as ten years. If a conscientious editor raised a query, he replied that everybody is as old as he feels. One of his favorite sayings was, *"Epater le bourgeois* is old hat. *Il faut le mystifier."* Mystification was as much second nature to him as pedantry to Burch. Harriet claimed that the best approximation to determine his real age was Newton's inverse square law: Petitjacques's appearance increased in youthfulness with the square of the distance. From the other end of the room he appeared to be under forty. The closer one got, the more parchmentlike the skin became, with a kind of tautness that gave the impression of plastic surgery.

His impromptu talk had indeed, as Blood had foreseen, the spicy ingredients and mushy consistency of a goulash sprinkled with hot curry. It gave Claire a craving for a toothpick. At the same time she began to be frightened. Petitjacques was preaching hatred in the name of love. As he warmed to his subject, the Mephistophelean charm gave way to bilious malice; a fine spray issued from his eloquent lips; he seemed to be literally spitting venom. In the name of peace he was declaring war against an undefined enemy. This enemy, to which he referred elusively as The System, seemed to change all the time its character and identity, from a mythological monster devouring its own children to a sociological abstraction somehow related to advertisements for washing machines in the mass media. This monster appeared to be wearing, at one and the same time, a steel helmet, a bowler hat and a mortarboard; he polluted the minds of young sociology students by teaching them History, and of budding sculptors by lessons in anatomy; he was a computerized Fascist Pig with a prenatal phobia of pubic hair (which, to the embryo, represents the hostile jungle); and he was a shameless hypocrite—"the hypocrisy of the system, *chers amis,* is epitomized by the monstrous segregation of public lavatories for men and women."

His talk was interstitched with such self-parodying remarks, yet there could be no doubt that his hatred of "the system"—of Western civilization in all its aspects—was genuine and obsessive. The system had to be destroyed in order to liberate society, and it could only be destroyed by all-out guerrilla war. An all-out guerrilla war did not require nuclear weapons. Its aim was the disintegration of the entire social fabric, fiber by fiber, until the streets were no longer safe for pedestrians sporting the conventional garbs of the system, until they would no longer dare to turn the ignition key in their cars for fear that it might activate a plastic bomb; nor board an airplane, for nobody could tell whether it would reach its destination, or any destination at all. Secretaries in big industrial firms would refuse to use typewriters for fear they might be booby-trapped; prosperous suburbanites would not dare to send their children to school for fear that they might be taken as hostages. The schools would have to close anyway, because teachers trying to teach "would be laughed in the face, if not punched in the nose and stripped *à poil,* to cure them of their public phobias." So-called crimes of violence would mount in curves steeper than a rocket take-off—not only such system-engendered crimes as burglary, but ritualized violence for its own sake, *l'art pour l'art.* The authorities would be helpless because you cannot stitch and patch up a rotten fabric in total disintegration. When the police hunt for a criminal, they look first of all for a motive; but you cannot hunt down killers who act without a motive, without any personal grudge against the victim who is merely a symbol of the system—not a person, but a thing . . . *"Mes amis,* you always forget what an extraordinarily remarkable thing it is that you can walk in a dark street past a person who could club you over the head just for the fun of it and never be found out. Why does he not do it? Because he is caught in the social fabric, a tight-woven web, a system, based on a tacit agreement, an implicit *contrat social,* which guarantees the security of Jean walking past Jacques in a dark street. It is not the police who protect him but the fabric, the tacit contract, for without it every Jacques and Jean would need his own bodyguard. So when the fabric of the system disintegrates into shreds, security disintegrates with it, and law and order all become an idyllic memory of the past. The aim of all-out guerrilla warfare, *chers amis,* is to complete this disintegration of the fabric which is already well on its way . . ."

When he had finished—abruptly, with an uncompleted sentence, as if he had suddenly got bored and saw no point in going on—there was an embarrassed silence. Niko was surprised to discover that his tough Call Girls were still capable of embarrassment. He glanced invitingly at several participants in turn, but nobody seemed anxious to speak; even Bruno merely shrugged his shoulders and gave a silent demonstration of washing his hands. At last Sir Evelyn, who during Petitjacques's lecture had pretended to be taking his afternoon nap, hands folded over his bulging stomach, seemed to rouse himself. "Mr. Chairman," he drawled plaintively, "I think we have heard all that odious flim-flam before, more than a century ago, from another crop of feeble-minded baboons, the Nihilists in the happy days of the Tsars. If Monsieur Petitjacques has ever heard the name of Feodor Mikhailovitch Dostoievski, 1821–1881, I would suggest he reads the novel *The Possessed,* and he will realize that the revolutionary message that he offers us consists of old chestnuts."

"Ah," said Petitjacques, regaining his mocking amiability, "you are quoting literature. I shall answer you with Antonin Artaud's irrefutable statement: 'The literature of the past was good enough for the past but is not good enough for the present.' "

Halder ruffled his mane with a gesture of despair. "Program!" he shouted at Petitjacques. "Your positive program! Drop-out, pop-out, shoot, hoot *in blinder Wut,* is not a program. You have been pulling legs."

"You do not understand," Petitjacques said patiently. "Our program is not to have a program. You can only advance if you do not know where you are going."

"Say that to a general."

"With generals we hold no *dialogue.*"

"Quatsch," Halder said feelingly; and there the discussion ended. For once the Call Girls were unanimous in their disapproval—and that, Claire thought, was perhaps the only point in Petitjacques's favor. There was a despair in his clowning, the desperation of the frenzied squirrel, which she found more frightening than Nikolai's lucid awareness of doom.

Solovief was just going to close the session, when Gustav noisily entered the conference room and announced, "Telegram for Herr Professor Kaletski." Having delivered it into Bruno's eager hands, he performed a semimilitary about-turn and left. There was a certain theatrical quality about the scene, and all eyes involuntarily turned on Bruno, as if receiving a telegram were a special event. But Bruno, a monument of imperturbable sang-froid, continued the elaborate operation of stuffing his attaché case with the litter of documents he had been reading during Petitjacques's talk (while politely cupping his ear with his free hand); and only when the operation was completed did he open the cable with a deft movement and a disparaging shrug. He seemed to take in the lengthy message at a single glance, and popped to his feet.

"One moment, Mr. Chairman, before we break up," he announced in a voice trembling with emotion. "I have just received a message which, I venture to say, may be of some interest to the participants of our conference. It has been addressed to me by a personality very close to the President of the United States of America—a personality whose identity I am not at liberty to disclose. The message reads as follows . . ."

Bruno's glance swept briefly but emphatically round the faces at the table, then along the auditors at the back wall.

Claire could not help suspecting that he had engineered beforehand Gustav's dramatic entrance.

"It reads as follows," Bruno repeated. " 'Professor Bruno Kaletski . . .' I will spare you the address, which incidentally the sender's secretary seems to have got slightly wrong—Schneehof instead of Schneedorf—otherwise the message would have reached us at the opening session, for which it was obviously intended . . . It reads: 'Am instructed to convey informally Mr. President's keen and agonized interest in outcome of your deliberations on quote approaches to survival unquote stop. In these critical days when future destiny of mankind at stake' —the text says 'shake' but the intended meaning is evident—repeat: 'when the destiny of mankind is at stake, the dedicated efforts of highpowered minds assembled at your conference may signify long overdue commencement of opening new avenues toward hopeful future stop please communicate soonest possible conclusions reached by your conference which will be given earnest consideration on highest level stop cordially. Signed . . .' " Abruptly Bruno sat down, as if to forestall an ovation.

And indeed, in the ensuing silence a faint clapping was heard. It was Miss Carey. One hand raised, she had cast a coy, questioning glance at Dr. Valenti, and seeing his encouraging smile, had engaged in this solo performance. It was rather like a demonstration of the old Zen *koan* about the one hand clapping. Everybody left hurriedly for the room next door, where the soothing cocktails were served.

Nikolai did not feel like having more than one cocktail; he and Claire were among the first in the dining room. They had unfolded their napkins when they saw Blood working his way down the spiral staircase and shuffling purposefully toward their table. He performed a surprisingly convincing imitation of a courtier's bow to Claire. "Are humble poets admitted to the Captain's table?"

"Pray be seated, Sir Evelyn," said Claire, returning the bow.

"My acute sense of observation has taught me," said Blood, lowering himself in slow motion into the chair next to hers, "that the prevailing etiquette of choosing one's table at interdisciplinary symposia is inspired by Charles Darwin's highly questionable theory which ascribes the progress of evolution to chance mutations. Those who adhere to this theory choose seats at random. They walk like somnambulists to the first empty chair in sight, regardless whether their neighbors happen to be neuropharmacologists or classical scholars, in the eternal, naïve hope of engaging in an interdisciplinary dialogue. Needless to say, the dialogue consists in exchanging asinine remarks about weather, health foods and slipped discs, whereafter they dry up and lapse into the strained silence of strangers on a train. It all goes to show that the *uomo universale* died with the Renaissance. What we have now is *Homo Babel*—each of us babbling away in his own specialized lingo on that presumptuous tower which is due to collapse any minute now."

"Rot," said Harriet, who had just come in, putting her stick under the table and sinking into the remaining empty chair. "You are plagiarizing John Donne's ' 'tis all in pieces, all coherence gone . . .' He was tearing his hair out just because Copernicus said the earth was not the center of the world . . ."

Blood eyed her with undisguised loathing. "Begging your forgiveness, gracious lady, Donne was right. Copernicus and his cronies started taking the cosmic jigsaw to pieces, and all the king's horses and all the king's men could not put it together again."

H.E. decided to ignore him, and turned to Nikolai. "What did you make of Bruno's *coup de théâtre*?"

Nikolai shrugged; he was using a delicious local bread-roll to model a creature that looked like a dinosaur. "It was difficult to take seriously, like everything else coming from Bruno. But that is just his personality. He does have real influence—after all, he is on the Advisory Board and so on. Up there, they do seem to take him seriously. God knows what their criteria of seriousness are."

"A bottle of Neuchâtel, *Schätzchen,*" Blood said to Mitzie, who was serving the thick pea soup, with chunks of sausage in it.

"Big bottle?" Mitzie asked.

"Indeed a full bottle, *Schätzchen.* You should know my little habits by now."

Nikolai ordered a carafe of the local red. "Just who or what is to be taken seriously?" he repeated belligerently.

"I have the doubtful privilege of having supped with many a politician," said Blood. "It goes with being a Call Girl laureate. I was never able to take any of them seriously—I mean as a human being—whatever that means. The power, yes; the person, no. They reminded me of performing seals in a circus, balancing balls on their snouts—balls filled with dynamite."

"You could use the same metaphor for scientists," said Nikolai. "When Einstein proclaimed the equivalence of energy and mass, nobody took it seriously, except as a feat of mental acrobatics—balancing abstract equations in the circus of science. Until he dropped the ball . . ."

Harriet, who had been engaged in a whispered conversation with Claire but had not missed a word, struck her glass with her dripping soup spoon. "If I can make any sense out of what you two are saying, you are both puzzled and embarrassed because some big brass, for some unknown reason, are apparently taking this conference *seriously.* Not dear little Bruno—*us.* But you are frightened to admit it."

"Hear, hear," said Claire.

"But my dear lady," sighed Blood, "I have never, never been able to take even myself seriously, so why should I not be frightened? My only courage consists in facing up to my cowardice."

Harriet again ignored him and turned on Nikolai. "Nikolai Borisovitch Solovief," she boomed, "Little Father, here is your chance. Is not that message the answer to your prayers? That letter to the President—now they seem to be begging for it."

"Hear, hear," said Claire, putting her hand lightly on Nikolai's shoulder, though she rarely indulged in demonstrative gestures of affection. "I agree with Harriet. Bruno may not be the hero of my dreams, but let us admit he is a godsend."

Nikolai shook his head. "I am looking for an explanation for this sudden interest in our moth-eaten assembly."

"I may offer a parable by way of explanation . . ." drawled Blood. "One of the most disreputable episodes in my life was a stretch of three months in Hollywood. To my mind there has always been a close resemblance between Hollywood and Washington, D.C. Both have the same atmosphere of publicity-seeking, intrigue, hysteria, jockeying for position, fawning to the gossip columnists, the same ambiance of recurrent crises. It was during such a crisis that I was called to the telephone in my London flat at the unearthly hour of six A.M. I thought it was one of my gay young friends informing me that he had just taken an overdose of sleeping pills—they love doing that—but no, it was the president of one of those mammoth companies whose name is a household word in the film world. I have never met him, but he took the liberty of addressing me by my first name, and practically sobbed on my shoulder across the transatlantic cable line. 'There is a CRISIS on,' he wailed, all Hollywood was shaken by the crisis, weeping and gnashing their teeth, and the box offices all over the world might as well close down. He went on to confess to me, confidentially and off the record: "It's all our fault, Evelyn, take my word for it or call me a liar, it's *our* fault because we kept to the beaten track and went on making TRASH instead of making ART. We gave the public plenty of CUNT, but what the box office is yelling for is ART. Now for making ART, Evelyn, we need TALENT. What Hollywood needs is not lousy scriptwriters chasing dollars, but TALENT—people like YOU. Not cheap hacks, but guys with a CREATIVE VISION . . .'

"Then he came to the point. To start the new era of ART they had decided to make a film on the life of 'that well-known English poet, Baron Byron. Sure you must have heard of him, Evelyn—George Gordon Noel Byron. Sixth Baron. He was a Lord too.' They'd had five scriptwriters on it, 'so-called top class,' one after another. No good. They didn't produce ART. 'So that's where you come in, Evelyn.'

"I told him, politely, to go and commit sodomy with himself. Then he named a figure and I withdrew my remark, and my cigarette burnt a hole in my pajamas . . ."

He acted the scene with a shaking hand, the other holding an imaginary telephone receiver. Even Harriet had to admit that, though loathsome, Blood could be quite funny. He finished abruptly: "End of parable. Washington, like Hollywood, is in a CRISIS. There is weeping and gnashing of teeth. The scriptwriters of history have turned out to be lousy hacks. So they are looking for fresh TALENT to save them—guys with a CREATIVE VISION. That's where you come in."

He sipped his glass of Neuchâtel, delicately balancing its stem between fat fingers, satisfied with the effect of his story.

"There may be something in it," said Nikolai slowly.

"It was a lovely parable," said Claire. "How did it end?"

"Somebody discovered that Byron had slept with his half-sister and had a queer streak to boot, so it was off. That was before the golden dawn of porn. Sounds incredible today. Anyway, they had to pay me. To compensate them for the loss, I wrote into the President's Golden Book the only rhymed couplet I have ever composed:

'I don't care a fart
For your notions of ART.' "

"That was in abominable taste," said Harriet. "You've spoilt your story."

"I always do that," said Blood. "It gives me a kind of masochistic pleasure."

Random events weave their own patterns. Late in the evening, Professor Burch and Dr. Horace Wyndham happened to be the only remaining guests in the cocktail room. Hansie and Mitzie had gone to bed, but there was a comforting array of bottles on the shelves, left at the free disposal of the Call Girls. It was a tradition which enlivened some though not all symposia, designed to facilitate interdisciplinary interrelationships.

Wyndham cautiously approached the bar—he seemed to walk on tiptoe—and helped himself to a sizable Scotch with water. Burch, sitting at the bar, was apparently immersed in correcting his galley proofs, with a half-finished highball at his elbow. Wyndham noticed that some of its contents had spilled onto the printed sheets, and that Burch's eyes behind the rimless glasses stared even more fishlike than usual. "Best moment of the day," Wyndham said with a sociable giggle.

Burch seemed to become belatedly aware of the other man's presence. "What do you mean by that?" he asked suspiciously.

"I mean," Wyndham beamed, taking a gulp of his Scotch, "what we euphemistically call a nightcap. I am afraid I am an incorrigible after-dinner drinker."

Burch considered the matter. "I prefer for relaxation an occasional sip of bourbon," he pronounced. "They don't have it here." He picked up his glass, and after a moment's reflection, emptied it as if it were water. A few more yellow drops appeared on the galleys.

Wyndham climbed onto the barstool and became appreciably taller; he had a well-built torso, only his legs were short. "I hope I am not interrupting your meditations," he said. Since he was nearer to the bottle, he filled up the glass which Burch absent-mindedly held out. Burch put some ice cubes into it, but ignored the soda bottle.

" 'Meditation' is not part of my vocabulary," he said.

"Call it contemplation," proposed Wyndham.

Burch shook his head, using more than the necessary amount of energy. "Nix," he said. "Soft-nosed terminology. We call it internalized verbal behavior, or subliminal vocalization, if you prefer it."

"I know," said Wyndham. "But we do not always think in articulate words."

"Nix," said Burch. "What you call thinking are inaudible vibrations of the vocal chords." He swirled the Scotch round the ice cubes, and drank it apparently without parting his lips. The liquid vanished between them as if by osmosis. Wyndham tried to visualize Burch in the act of love, and quickly took a gulp.

"Children," Burch unexpectedly blurted out. "Kids. You a pediatrician?"

"Sort of. Infants are more in my line. Tots."

"Tots become kids. Kids grow up . . . It's only natural," Burch added reflectively, as if to reassure himself.

"Do you have children?"

Burch nodded, again too energetically, and stared into his glass. Wyndham guessed what was coming.

"Two," said Burch.

"Well, did you try your educational engineering on them?" Wyndham tittered. "To 'predict and control' their behavior?"

"Sure." Burch nodded again and finished his glass. Wyndham officiated with the bottle for both of them. "Sure," Burch repeated. "You a pediatrician. Maybe you have an explanation. Boy, Hector junior, twenty-one. Did brilliantly at Harvard Law School. Year ago started on hashish. Six months ago on heroin. Twice hospitalized. Psychotic episodes. Two of his buddies committed suicide. One from a railway bridge. Girl, Jenny, seventeen. Did brilliantly at high school. Fell for a pop guitarist. Followed the group everywhere through the United States of America. Made plaster casts first of guitarist's penis, then of the others' too. Became a sort of specialty with her. Mrs. Burch discovered Jenny's collection of casts during a search in her cupboard. Quite a collection . . . I guess it's only natural. Sexual behavior has many variables. Hindus have lingams in their temples. No value judgments intended, but it seems slightly odd. You a pediatrician . . ."

"Won't you have a little soda in your glass?" Wyndham said conversationally.

"Only blows you up . . . I asked you questions. What's the explanation?"

"My line are babies in cradles. Not adolescents."

"Maybe it's the influence of Mrs. Burch. Mrs. Burch is a Catholic convert. Believes in all the mumbo-jumbo. Attends mass. Attends spiritualist séances too. Apparently Great Chief Chingakook wised her up about Jenny's collection, over the ouija board."

"Most families have their upsets. Perhaps they'll settle

down," Wyndham said soothingly. He, too, began to feel the liquor, and Burch's revelations, combined with the effects of the *Höhenluft,* made him feel somewhat odd.

"It must be the unscientific influence of Mrs. Burch," Professor Burch mused. "Pavlov's method of paradoxical conditioning turned his dogs into neurotics. When you condition a subject in two mutually contradictory ways, he is liable to go to pieces."

"They'll settle down," Wyndham repeated, sliding down from his high stool. "I wouldn't worry. In the meantime, thank you for an interesting conversation."

"Haven't answered my questions," Burch protested, fingering his empty glass.

"And so to bed," Wyndham said cheerfully. "Perhaps we ought to turn the lights out." He extended a helping hand as Burch scrambled to his feet. Walking out through the glass door on slightly unsteady legs, they gave the impression of Mr. Punch helping the Sergeant Major off the parade ground.

Wednesday

On the third day of the Symposium, the keenly awaited duel between Otto von Halder and Harriet Epsom took its predictable course. It was not their first confrontation; in fact, they had met and fought twice already in that same year—at an ecology congress at Mexico City and a futurology symposium at the Academy in Stockholm.

Halder spoke in the morning. It had to be admitted that his delivery was impressive, although the paper he read was essentially the same—except for a few paraphrases and impromptus—which he had given in Stockholm and in Mexico; nor did he seem in the least embarrassed by the fact that Harriet had been present on both occasions, since he expected, not without justification, that she too would come up with a slightly paraphrased repeat performance. After all, one could not expect scientists to produce some original discovery on each of these public occasions. Rather, they looked upon themselves as a traveling team of professional wrestlers, who are familiar with one another's antics and go through their paces, each time pretending surprise and indignation at the base tricks of their opponents.

Halder's thesis was basically that of the prophets of Old

Testament, from Isaiah to Jeremiah; his flowing white mane and the pathos of his delivery confirmed this impression. Man, in his view, was a species of assassins—*Homo homicidus*. This was his principal characteristic. Other animals only kill prey belonging to a different species. A hawk killing a field mouse can hardly be accused of murder. The law of the jungle permits feeding on other species but forbids slaying members of one's own. *Homo homicidus* is the only offender against this law—a victim of endemic aggressiveness directed at his own kin; a bundle of murderous instincts . . .

"Rot," Harriet remarked.

"Ach so?" Halder replied with an exaggerated shrug. "You will have your say later. Now it is my say. And I say to you, who is a zoologist, show me any other animal who murders and slaughters its con-specifics—its own biological kin. Yes, animals also have conflicts—over territory, or sexual competition, or food, or wanting to be the boss. They fight, but with gloves, like boxers. They always stop short of killing. It is a ritual—like fencing with the *épée*. It *looks* savage, but it is all bluff and bluster, and when one combatant signals '*touché*,' the other stops. The wolf or the dog signals *touché* by lying down on its back, paws in the air" (Halder mimicked the waving of paws); "the fish swims away, the stag slinks away" (Halder grew antlers with his fingers and made slinking motions). "And the victor lets him get away. But man—tsh sht . . ." (he indicated cutting the throat of poor Tony, who sat next to him). "Tschsht—kill for money, kill for jealousy, kill for power, kill for territory . . ."

He ruffled his white hair in despair. How was *Homo homicidus* to be prevented from destroying himself? From committing geno-suicide? He raised both arms in a prophetic gesture:

> *"Gefährlich ist's den Leu zu wecken*
> *Verderblich ist des Tigers Zahn;*

Jedoch der Schrecklichste der Schrecken,
Das ist der Mensch in seinem Wahn . . .

"As Friedrich von Schiller tells us:

" 'Tis dangerous to wake the lion
Dangerous is the tiger's tooth
But most horrible of all horrors
Is man in his madness—forsooth . . ."

There were several repressed giggles.

"Ach so," said Halder, controlling his anger. "You think it is funny? But whatever you think, the killer instinct is a scientific fact, it is in our flesh and blood, under the skin, it is in you and me. If we deny it, if we do not dare to face the facts about our own nature, then there is no hope for a remedy . . ."

He was interrupted by Petitjacques. "Program," he shouted. "Your positive program. That is what you asked me yesterday."

"And you said your program is not to have a program. My program is to have a program. But we are only at the beginning of learning the lessons which science teaches us. And science teaches us that all other animals except man do not kill their own kind because their combats are *ritualized,* mock combats, play-acting. Therefore, the logical remedy for man is also to *ritualize* his aggression, to canalize his killer instinct into symbolic displays. Thus we could transform *Homo homicidus* into *Homo ludens,* the playing animal, who abreacts his killer instinct in dramatic but harmless rituals like two stags staging a duel but never hitting, as you say, below the belt . . ."

Now Halder got into his stride. Yes, indeed he had a program, he assured M. Petitjacques, and it went under the simple name AA—Aggression-Abreaction—as already briefly described in his recent book. Abreaction therapy was as old as mankind. From *The Bacchae* of Euripides we learn how the Theban women worked themselves into a frenzy and symbolically tore the horned god to pieces. After that ecstasy, they stopped nagging their husbands. In the Dark Ages there were flagellants and tarantula dancers who worked off their aggression by masochistic practices, but even these were better than repressing aggression until it burst its dams. Much better were the jousting bouts and splendid tournaments, which resembled the ritualized duels of stags. And in modern times came sport—soccer, rugby, boxing, fencing—all splendid, harmless outlets for the killer instinct . . .

But this turned out not to be enough. More efficient abreaction techniques were needed. Some very sensible psychiatrists in the United States cured their patients by simply teaching them to be rude. Halder picked up a book and read with much feeling a passage he had marked: " 'Tell people all the time what you think of them, regardless of whether it's politic or impolitic. Down with Emily Post! Live with the shades up. Get the steam out! Be an emotional broadcaster, not a receiver. Never play another person's game. Play your own.' I am quoting the book of an excellent American therapist, speaking to one of his patients. To another one he speaks even more forcefully: 'Never be reasonable about anything. Get rid of your irritations. Don't keep your feelings corked up, any more than you would your stomach. Yelling gets the knot out of your gut. Remember, they that spit shall inherit the earth.' "

He paused for effect. "I am glad to say that the author has a considerable following in his country. But acting on the individual plane is not enough . . ."

In the remaining fifteen minutes of his lecture, Halder developed his grandiose projects—foreshadowed in *Homo Homicidus*—for creating outlets for violence on a mass scale. It would start in the kindergarten, where all-in wrestling would be made compulsory. The much-maligned dueling fraternities of German universities would be revived—Halder fingered lovingly two horizontal scars on his right cheek. Future mass entertainments would include gladiatorial games, athletes fighting robots programmed to hurt but not to kill. On an even larger scale, realistic war games could be held every year in summer—the notorious rioting season—with whole armies engaged in repelling hostile invading forces, also composed of manlike robots made of software and programmed to bleed profusely. Lastly, Halder wished to remind his dear colleagues of the daily Hate Sessions and quarterly Hate Weeks in George Orwell's novel *1984*. The author himself obviously regarded them as a damnable institution, invented by Big Brother. But there was another way of looking at the matter. Listen to this . . .

Halder picked up another book, lying in front of him, with a marker in it. He read aloud:

" 'Before the Hate had proceeded for thirty seconds, uncontrollable exclamations of rage were breaking out from half of the people in the room . . . In its second minute the Hate rose to a frenzy. People were leaping up and down in their places and shouting at the tops of their voices . . . In a lucid moment Winston found that he was shouting with the others and kicking his heel violently against the rung of his chair. The horrible thing about the Two Minutes Hate was not that one was obliged to act a part, but, on the contrary, that it was impossible to avoid joining in. Within thirty seconds any pretence was always unnecessary. A hideous ecstasy of fear and vindictiveness, a desire to kill, to torture, to smash faces in with a sledge-hammer, seemed to flow through the whole group of people like an electric current, turning one even against one's will into a grimacing, screaming lunatic. And yet the rage that one felt was an abstract, undirected emotion which could be switched from one object to another like the flame of a blowlamp . . . It was even possible, at moments, to switch one's hatred this way or that by a voluntary act.' "

Halder put the book down. "Here you have the classic abreaction therapy on a mass scale. The Orphic mystery cult revived. When the Hate Session is finished, the people are exhausted. The thirst for violence is assuaged. The killer instinct has found its symbolic fulfillment. They have obtained *katharsis,* they feel purified. Mr. Orwell got it all wrong. He hated the Hate idea because he was a good hater himself; otherwise he would not have been able to give such a vivid description of the scene, but his theoretical interpretation of it was wrong. He was describing a session of mass therapy without knowing it. But at least in one very advanced industrial country Mr. Orwell's message—or perhaps Otto von Halder's message—has been correctly interpreted and put into beneficial practice. I shall now quote to you a recent news report from a well-known American weekly magazine:

" '*Therapy by Dummies.* Leaving his station, the distraught worker approaches two life-sized padded dummies seated on a platform. Picking up a bamboo stave placed conveniently near by, he ferociously attacks the dummies, slashing and swatting them until his fury is spent. This strange activity, repeated daily at an Osaka plant of the giant Matsushita Electric Industrial Co., is actually a form of therapy provided by Board Chairman Konosuke Matsushita as a rather uncommon fringe benefit. In Matsushita's "self-control room," which has attracted thousands of workers, an employee can harmlessly work off his tension, frustration and rage.'

"Mr. Chairman, there was a suggestion that this conference should make concrete proposals to certain exalted personages in your country concerning the strategy of survival. I think in all humility"—at the word humility a giggle or two could be heard—"in all humility, that my presentation contains relevant pointers towards such a strategy, and towards the contents of the intended message . . ."

"It is getting worse, *caro* Guido," Claire wrote, "and I cannot help thinking of Juvenal: 'Why do I write satire?' he asks. 'Say rather how could I help it?' Niko is blaming himself for having selected the wrong people, and even I, faithful and loyal Claire, am beginning to wonder? He wanted to avoid the stuffed shirts, the complacent establishment pundits, and collect the more lively ones among the international Call Girl set, known for their provocative ideas. When you read their stuff or get them alone in a relaxed mood, you realize their qualities—but the moment you put them together in a conference room, they behave like schoolboys performing a solemn play. They are worse than politicians, because politicians are ham actors by natural disposition, whereas most academics seem to suffer from arrested emotional development. Politicians take their pride in making impassioned speeches and indulging in rhetorical flights; scientists pose as dispassionate servants of Truth, free from all emotional bias, while ambition and jealousy steadily gnaw away their entrails. And what is their Truth, *caro* Guido, what is Truth? It seems to me that each of them possesses a small fragment of the Truth which he believes to be the Whole Truth, which he carries around in his pocket like a tarnished bubble gum, and blows up on solemn occasions to prove that it contains the ultimate mystery of the universe. Discussion? Interdisciplinary dialogue? There is no such thing, except on the printed program. When the dialogue is supposed to start, each gets his own bubble gum out and blows it into the others' faces. Then they repair, satisfied, to the cocktail room.

"Take our dear Otto von Halder, of international fame,

who was blowing his gum this morning. It was a re-hash of his latest book, which has created such a scandal, with some more hair-raising embellishments added. I suppose there is a grain of truth in his ideas—the simple little truth that letting steam off is better than overheating the boiler. It is almost a truism, but he blew it until it became inflated into a grotesque kind of religion, with echoes of Black Mass and the Nuremberg Rallies. Incidentally, Otto *was* a member of the Nazi Party—everybody knows it, but pretends not to know. He played no active part; he simply had to join, otherwise his career would have been ruined. Or is that an insufficient excuse? He also sheltered a couple of Jewish colleagues, risking his neck. Or is that not enough? There is no end to these conundrums—the snares of the past. I would not have brought the subject up, had it not been at the back of everybody's mind—rightly or wrongly, I cannot decide. It may have something to do with the *genius loci*. Behind each yodel there is the echo of a *Heil* . . . ?

"The discussion was a mess, as the previous ones had been. Harriet was holding her horses for the afternoon session, when it was to be her turn to perform. Wyndham, with much tittering, denied any evidence of the killer instinct in babes in the cradle. He was pooh-poohed by Otto and challenged by the Kleinian female to a sort of verbal ping-pong match which lasted the rest of the session. Bruno, who had been sharpening his knife all morning, waiting for the opportunity to move in for the kill, was at the critical moment called to the telephone for a transatlantic palaver; and as the Fräuleins at various exchanges kept cutting him off, he missed the rest of the session.

"It is all very frustrating. I feel sorry for Niko. He foresaw it, of course, in the cynical half of his divided heart; in the other half he keeps a niche for miracles. So far none have transpired . . ."

In the afternoon it was Harriet Epsom's turn. Her way of reading her prepared paper contrasted strangely with her ebullient private manner: she spoke in a dry, schoolmasterly voice, as if addressing a student seminar. She started by confessing some bewilderment about an apparent reversal of roles: Professor von Halder, an eminent anthropologist, had based his thesis mainly on arguments borrowed from zoology—predator and prey, ritualized combat, defense of territory and so on; whereas she herself, a humble zoologist, was mainly interested in those specific attributes which were characteristic of man—and of man alone. But this reversal of roles seemed to her typical of the *Zeitgeist:* anthropologists, as well as psychologists, seemed to be determined to ignore the humanity of man, and to build their theories of human nature on analogies derived from zoology—Pavlov's dogs, Professor Burch's rats, Konrad Lorenz's geese. In mock bewilderment, Harriet just wondered, wide-eyed, what had got into them . . .

Halder was listening impassively, sitting sideways in his chair, offering Harriet the view of his noble profile. Burch was demonstratively correcting his galley proofs; Bruno was busily taking notes; Blood was somnolescent. Petitjacques was absent.

However, Harriet continued soberly, if animals can teach us something about our own nature, then surely we must turn our attention not to rats or geese but to those species that are nearest to us, such as apes and monkeys. Some forty years ago, zoologists like Zuckerman who made systematic studies of the behavior of primates in zoological gardens, came up with conclusions that seemed to support von Halder's pessimistic views of the congenital aggressivity of our species, for these monkeys were highly irritable, constantly bickering and fighting, obsessed with sex, and ruled by murderously violent bosses. But it turned out that to generalize from the behavior of monkeys in unnaturally crowded conditions of confinement was as hazardous as it would be to describe human society in terms of the behavior of prisoners in a concentration camp. A new generation of field naturalists—the Carpenters, Washburns, Goodalls, Shallers and Imanishies—who had spent years of their lives observing various species of monkeys in the wild, came up with a quite different picture. They unanimously affirmed that free-living primate societies are peaceful, and that there is an almost complete absence of serious fighting, either within the band or between bands. Aggressive behavior makes its appearance only when tensions of one kind or another put the animals under stress—as in the zoo cage. There was no sign—not the faintest trace—of von Halder's killer instinct to be found in our ancestors . . .

Halder interrupted, "So it is a unique property of man, as I have said."

"Rot," said Harriet, momentarily relapsing into her usual style. "There is not a trace of evidence for a killer instinct either in monkey or in man. Violence is not a biological drive, but a reaction provoked by stress when it exceeds a critical limit."

"So wars do not exist," remarked Halder.

"They do exist, but they are not the result of individual aggressiveness. Any historian will tell you that the number of individuals murdered for personal motives was always negligible compared to the millions murdered in the name of impersonal causes: tribal loyalty, patriotism, Christian against Moslem, Protestant against Catholic, and so on. Freud proclaimed *ex cathedra* that wars were caused by pent-up aggressive instincts in search of an outlet, and people believed him because it made them feel guilty. But he did not produce a shred of historical or psychological evidence for his claim. Soldiers do not hate. They are frightened, bored, sex-starved, homesick; they fight with resignation, because they have no other choice, or with enthusiasm for King and Country, the righteous cause, the true religion—moved not by hatred but *by loyalty*. Homicide committed for selfish motives is a statistical rarity in all cultures. Homicide for unselfish motives is the dominant phenomenon of man's history. His tragedy is not an excess of aggression, but an excess of devotion. If you replace the label *Homo homicidus* by *Homo fidelis,* you get nearer to the truth. It is loyalty and devotion which make the fanatic . . ."

"So fanatics don't hate," remarked von Halder with a sigh of resignation in the face of such unwisdom.

"They do hate, but it is an impersonal and unselfish hatred of everything which threatens the object of their devotion. They hate not qua individuals, but qua members of the group—tribe, nation, Church, party, what-have-you. Their aggressivity is loyalty turned upside down."

"But I can turn your sentence also upside down," said Halder. "What you call loyalty is nothing but aggression standing on its head."

"Rot," said Harriet. "That kind of dialectic you can leave to Monsieur Petitjacques."

"I would not entirely dissent from Herr von Halder's view," chimed in the voice of Helen Porter from the outer perimeter of the conference room.

"No, you wouldn't," Harriet rasped. "Snakes in the grass are not qualified to make pronouncements about loyalty."

"According to von Halder's view," said Wyndham with an apologetic titter, "the act of love is an act of inverted aggression, and the male organ an aggressive weapon."

"But of course it is," said Helen earnestly. "That isn't much of a joke, you know."

For some reason this caused a protracted outburst of hilarity, in which Harriet and Halder also participated. Blood looked at the assembly with baleful eyes. "Schoolboys will be schoolboys," he remarked darkly.

Harriet resumed her argument with an attack on another fashionable theory which Halder had played up: that the origin of war could be found in the biological urge displayed by some animals to defend at all costs their own stretch of land or water. It was, she contended, a thoroughly misleading analogy. The wars of men, with rare exceptions, were not fought for the individual ownership of bits of space. The man who goes to war actually abandons his home and family which he is supposed to defend, and does his shooting far away from them; and what makes him do it is not the biological urge to defend his personal acreage of farmland or meadows, but —to say it once more—his devotion to symbols derived from tribal lore, divine commandments and sacred causes. Wars were fought not for territory, but for words.

"*Ach so.* You mentioned flags. Now it is words."

"Flags are optical slogans. Anthems are musical slogans. But man's deadliest weapon is language. He is as susceptible to being hypnotized by slogans and symbols as he is to infectious diseases. And when there is an epidemic, the group mind takes over. It obeys its own rules, which are different from the rules of conduct of individuals. When a person identifies himself with a group, his critical faculties are diminished and his passions enhanced by a kind of emotive resonance. The individual is not a killer; the group is; and by identifying with it, the individual becomes one. This is the infernal dialectic reflected in man's history. The egotism of the group feeds on the altruism of its members; the savagery of the group feeds on the devotion of its members. The worst of madmen is a saint run mad, as one of our poets said . . ."

"Blake?" ventured Tony, who had sat as still as a little mouse.

"Pope," grunted Blood. "He had his moments."

"To conclude, Mr. Chairman," said Harriet. "It seems to me that the disasters of our history are mainly due to our irresistible urge to become identified with a group, nation, Church or what have you, and to espouse its beliefs uncritically and enthusiastically. If Dr. Valenti and his colleagues could come up with some synthetic enzyme which would make man immune against suggestibility by slogans, the demagogues would go out of business, and half the battle for survival would be won. Valenti and his friends have given us drugs for brainwashing, to induce hallucinations and psychotic states at will. Now they should concentrate on the opposite task and find a paregoric which makes sailors immune against the siren's song and the masses against the barking of politicians. When they have found it, let them put it into the tap water, like the chlorine which protects us against typhoid and whatnot. I am serious. If the big brass want our advice, this is what I would tell them. Everything else is rot."

There were beads of sweat on Harriet's powdered brow and upper lip. She had worked herself into a kind of controlled fury which had stopped even Halder's ironic interruptions. Claire, sitting behind her with the other auditors, leaned forward and patted Harriet's bare and ample shoulder.

After a few seconds' silence, Dr. Valenti lifted a well-manicured hand, but Bruno got in first. He had missed his chance in the morning session to demolish Halder, but Harriet as a target would do just as well. He was not sure, he informed Mr. Chairman, whether Dr. Epsom had spoken in earnest, or, to put it in a different way, whether she had intended her proposal to be taken into serious consideration . . .

"You bet I did," snapped Harriet.

In that case, continued Bruno, he would venture to remind his illustrious colleagues of his own modest contribution to the opening discussion, its traces still visible on the blackboard, which nobody had bothered to erase. The vertical dividing line he had chalked on the board, to symbolize the assembly's split mind, was still there, and also the words CONTROLLED SCHIZOPHRENIA–NO OFFENSE; and SUB SP. AET.–TOMORROW ! ? Bruno stabbed at each of them with a piece of chalk. He was sorry, nay distressed, to have to remind the conference of his warning against the dangers of falling into one of two opposite errors: (a) complacent aloofness, *versus* (b) panic and hysteria. Dr. Epsom's appeal to the pharmacological industry to solve the problems of mankind appeared to him as an example of (b)—but while his lips smoothly uttered this damning phrase, his right hand pointed at the words NO OFFENSE. Taking into account both the predicament of mankind in general which the day's two speakers had described in such eloquent, albeit biased, terms—his hand pointed again—and in particular the conflicts currently raging in the Near, Middle and Far East, with their imminent threat of escalation—regarding which he had received some confidential information just an hour ago; taking into consideration both the long-term problems and the acute crises, it seemed to him more important than ever to keep a cool head and arrive at judgments and recommendations—if recommendations there were to be—which struck a measured balance between detached reasoning and vigorous action. Such action, however, must assign first priority to measures designed to enhance mutual understanding between governments and nations by means of increasing the information flow through the national and international agencies instituted for that purpose . . .

"Information flow regulated by appropriate feedback mechanisms," John D. John interjected earnestly.

"Quite right. We are, however, fortunate enough to dispose of some feedback mechanisms in our electoral system, the various advisory bodies assisting government, and international bodies such as the Security Council and the United Nations Educational, Scientific and Cultural Organization, commonly referred to as UNESCO . . ."

Solovief rapped the table. "Excuse me, Bruno, but you have said all this during our first discussion, and you will have the opportunity on Friday . . ."

Kaletski froze, the chalk still in his raised hand. He looked pathetic and contrite—the prodigy stopped in the act of showing off. "Sorry, Niko," he said quite humbly, "one does get so carried away . . ." They all had a feeling of *déjà vu.*

Solovief was unmoved. "I think Dr. Valenti had something to say."

Valenti rose in a single, smooth movement. "All I would like to say at this stage is that I agree with the main points of Dr. Epsom's diagnosis. I hope you will allow me to entertain you on Friday with a little experiment that seems to speak in favor of it." He sat down as gracefully as he had got up.

Blood gave a kind of grunt. "Don't see why you have to be so bloody enigmatic."

Valenti smiled at him agreeably, but said nothing.

It was Wyndham's turn to raise a pudgy hand. He declared himself to be in agreement with much of what Harriet had said. He too believed that aggressivity was a stress reaction, not a primary instinct. He too agreed with the necessity of making a distinction between personal behavior, which under normal conditions was by and large peaceful, and group behavior, which was dominated by emotions and tended to affirm, in aggressive ways, the group's customs, traditions, language and beliefs, rejecting with passionate scorn the customs and beliefs of all others. This paradox was perhaps the main reason why the human race had made such a mess of its history. But where was one to look for the roots of the paradox? Dr. Epsom had singled out as a primary cause man's suggestibility—his readiness to accept the traditions and beliefs of the group and become hypnotized by them. At this point he, Wyndham, had a further hypothesis to offer. The human infant had to endure a longer period of helplessness and dependence than the young of any other species. One might speculate that this early experience of total dependence was at least partly responsible for the tendency of our species to submit to authority, whether it was wielded by individuals or groups, and its suggestibility by doctrines and symbols . . . "Brainwashing starts in the cradle," Wyndham concluded with an apologetic giggle.

Unexpectedly, Burch concurred. It was, he said, a great satisfaction for him that "the eminent pediatrician," as he called Wyndham, realized the importance of early conditioning—and thus, by implication, subscribed to the doctrine of social engineering—in other words, the prediction and control of human behavior by positive and negative reinforcements. But he was interrupted by von Halder, suddenly shouting in Latin: *"Quis custodiet ipsos Custodes?* Who will control your controllers and engineer your engineers?"

Burch, John D. John, Jr., and Harriet all talked heatedly at the same time. Miss Carey shook her gray bun in despair and fiddled with the tape recorder's dials.

Solovief rapped the table with his lighter. His deep bass took over. "Professor Burch seems to have misunderstood the two previous speakers. Harriet and Wyndham did not wish to improve early conditioning, but to abolish it. Put it this way: the first suggestion the hypnotizer imposes on the subject is that he should be open to the hypnotizer's suggestions. The subject is being conditioned to become susceptible to conditioning. The helpless baby is put in the same position. It is turned into a willing recipient of beliefs. The actual belief system which is then shoved down its throat is a matter of chance. The hazards of birth alone determine the newborn's ethnic and religious loyalties; never mind on which number the roulette ball settles, he must live and die for that number. *Pro patria mori dulce et decorum est,* whichever the *patria* into which the stork dropped you. Halder says man's tragedy is to be a born killer. Harriet says his tragedy is to be a glutton for credos for which he must kill and get killed in unselfish devotion . . ."

"I wonder," Tony blurted out, blushing, "whether devotion is such a dirty word as Dr. Epsom makes it out to be."

"None of your holy eyewash," growled Blood.

"Do I have to dot my *i*'s for the sake of juveniles?" Harriet snapped at Tony. "I was talking of *misguided* devotion. But, to quote this abominable Halder, who is the custodian of the guides? Who decides whose is the right and whose the wrong devotion? The Irish Catholics or the Irish Protestants? Indians or Pakistanis? Trotskyists or Stalinists? The devotee is father to the fanatic."

"You mean," Tony ventured, "that the criteria of logical judgment do not apply, because devotion and loyalty are guided by emotion and not by reasoned argument?"

"I am glad the penny has dropped at last," said Harriet.

Blood gave one of his rhino-like grunts. "I smell a rat," he announced. "There is an unholy plot being hatched to vaccinate the newborn against the virus of belief. Will you need separate vaccines against tribalism, fetishism, Maoism, perchance aestheticism?"

"Buffoon," Harriet said contemptuously.

"I would have thought," giggled Wyndham, "that a single vaccine would be enough."

"And pray, what would it do? Abolish faith, loyalty and passion, turn us into computerized robots?"

"On the contrary, dear sir," Dr. Valenti said soothingly. "What we are earnestly searching for is a method to eliminate the schizophrenic condition reflected in mankind's deplorable history, or, to express it in your terminology, to reconcile the separate and hostile domains of passion and reason."

"You frighten me," growled Blood. "By Priapus, you do—though it must be admitted that I frighten easily. You may regard this as a personal aside, or a statement on behalf of that other culture which I have the doubtful honor to represent here. However, on one point at least I find myself in agreement with our formidable Dr. Epsom: wars are fought for words. That was neatly put. As a professional juggler with words, I am aware that they are man's most deadly weapon. I need not remind you of that maniac with the Chaplin mustache, a native of these bucolic regions, whose words were more powerful agents of destruction than thermonuclear bombs; or of the chain reaction which the words of a certain shopkeeper in Mecca released from Asia to the Atlantic. The word Allah consists of three phonemes and has caused so far an estimated thirty million deaths, with more to come. If you are making an inventory of the causes of the human predicament, you must give top priority to language. It is the heady poison which destroys our species."

"So we must abolish language," Halder said, slapping his knee in merriment. "We must include that proposition in our message."

"But that message," said Tony, "was delivered long ago: 'Let your communication be Yea, yea; Nay, nay; for anything beyond that cometh from the devil.' Matthew five, thirty-seven." He blushed again, as if he had uttered an obscenity.

"Well roared, lion," said Blood, glancing at Tony with pink lover's eyes.

"As a matter of fact," Solovief broke in, "mankind renounced language a long time ago—if by language you mean a method of communication for the whole species. Other species do possess a single system of communication by sign, sound or odor, which is understood by all its members. Dolphins travel a lot, but when they meet a stranger in the ocean they need no interpreter. Mankind is split into three thousand different language groups. Each language acts as a cohesive force within the group and as a divisive force between groups. Maharat hates Gujurat, Walloon despises Fleming, upper-class Englishman sneers at dropped aitches, and friend Blood detests our jargon . . ."

Language, he continued, seemed to be the main agency that made the disruptive forces triumph over the cohesive forces throughout the history of the species. One might even ask whether the term "species" was applicable to man. Halder had pointed out that animals had a built-in inhibition against killing con-specifics; yet it might be argued that Greeks killing Barbarians, Moors slaughtering Christian dogs, Nazis exterminating *Untermenschen* did not consider their victims to be members of their own species. Man displayed much greater variety in physique and behavior than any other creature—except for the products of artificial breeding—and language, instead of bridging over these differences, erected further barriers. It was significant that in an age when communication satellites made it possible for a message to be heard by the entire planet, there existed no planet-wide language which could also make it understood. It seemed even more paradoxical that the various international bodies, mentioned by Professor Kaletski, had never discovered that the simplest way to promote understanding was to promote a language that was understood by all . . .

Kaletski's right hand shot into the air. "If I may interrupt, Mr. Chairman, we have a subcommittee . . ."

"You have a subcommittee," Solovief boomed, "for studying the possibilities of an improved Esperanto which last met eighteen months ago, and was unable to agree whether its proceedings should be conducted in English or in French."

"Then you are better informed than I am," said Bruno, peeved. "I can assure you that I shall make inquiries into the matter at the proper quarters."

"Good luck," said Niko.

Blood raised the predictable objection that he did not intend to read Verlaine in Esperanto; Solovief reassured him that he need not worry, quoting as a precedent the happy coexistence of native vernaculars and Latin as a *lingua franca* in medieval Europe.

He went on to say that if a message was to emanate from the conference, it should urge that the matter be given high priority on the international agenda. Even the most awkward customers in the United Nations would have to agree that a shared world needed a shared language.

And there the discussion ended for the day.

"Today was a little better?" Claire wrote. "At least Niko is again taking an active interest, though it is difficult to see how seriously he—and the others—take the whole enterprise. Some bits and pieces emerged during the discussion, small parts of the jigsaw which is meant to show *what ails Man,* but they do not add up to much, or am I too dumb? Or is the patient suffering from as many different diseases as there are diagnosticians? Niko talked about the need for a language understood by all nations, but we do not even have a language which would enable specialists in different fields to understand each other.

"The news from Asia is frightening. On the brink once more. A small fringe benefit: the tourists are packing their bags and the mountains are less crowded. Always look on the sunny side of things—that's Claire, yours truly . . ."

She never mentioned in her letters the boy in the paddy-field, whose image haunted Niko and her—like a pain which one sometimes forgot, but which was always there. They generally avoided talking about it.

Thursday

Professor Burch's lecture on Thursday morning was a fiasco. Niko might have cunningly hoped that this would happen, but now he regretted having invited him. And yet Burch occupied one of the most coveted chairs in the United States; his textbooks were mandatory reading, and the particular brand of psychology which he represented had recently been shown, by a nation-wide poll among students, to be by far the most popular.

His lecture was called The Technology of Behavior and most of his time was taken up by showing lantern slides of rats in boxes learning to press a lever to obtain a food pellet, and of pigeons being trained to strut around in figures of eight. The reward was called a positive reinforcer, withholding the reward a negative reinforcer; the rate at which the creatures responded was recorded by electronic equipment, and the whole procedure was called operant conditioning. At the first mention of this term Blood gave a leonine yawn and Niko gently rapped the table. In the last three minutes of his talk Burch proclaimed, without further ado, that the method he had demonstrated was applicable, with only minor technical modifications, to the control of human behavior—which obeyed the same elementary laws as that of pigeons and rats. All that the technology of behavior needed to solve the problems of mankind were scientifically controlled schedules of positive and negative reinforcements. To talk about good or bad, freedom, dignity and purpose was antiquated poppycock. If a message was to be sent to the White House, it should strongly recommend that the teaching machines invented by Professor Skinner, the founder of behavioral engineering, should be made mandatory in schools on an international scale, and their programming be done in the international language advocated by Professor Solovief.

At the end of the lecture, only one pair of hands was heard clapping, those of John D. John, Jr. Blood, slumped in his chair, said in a somnolent voice, "In my salad days, as an undergrad much in demand, I did some slumming—listened to lectures in biology. In those days it was fashionable to warn students against the heresy of anthropomorphism, of attributing human thoughts and feelings to animals. Now Burch is preaching to us the opposite heresy—that we should not attribute to man thoughts and feelings which are not demonstrable in his rats. As my favorite writer said somewhere, the pundits of Burch's school have replaced the anthropomorphic view of the rat with a ratomorphic view of man. I am surprised they are not growing whiskers."

"The rudeness of Dr. Blood," said Burch with commendable restraint, "indicates that in his early youth he was exposed to a schedule of negative reinforcers."

"But I liked the stick and disliked carrots," said Blood. "What do you make of that?"

"Human nature is unfathomable," giggled Wyndham. Burch shrugged in silence and there, to everybody's relief, the discussion came to an end.

During the lunch break, the newly installed air-raid siren had a trial run. Its purpose seemed questionable to the natives of Schneedorf, who did not believe that anybody would be interested in dropping a bomb on their village—except for the people in the rival skiing resort of Schneeberg, on the other side of the valley, who spoke a different, abominable dialect, but fortunately possessed no bombs. Besides, the village of Schneedorf had its powerful church bells, whose message, when there was a fire, could be heard in the remotest farm; and each farmstead had its own picturesque belfry, which could be reactivated should the church bells go *kaputt.* But the government in its wisdom had ordered that every hamlet should be equipped with a siren; and there it was, installed in the fire brigade's tower out of the taxpayers' money. Nevertheless, it was a special occasion; the members of the voluntary fire brigade had turned out in their becoming uniforms, and so had the Herr Pfarrer, the burgomaster, the Kongresshaus Gustav, and some other V.I.P.s. The burgomaster was the village blacksmith, a moronic giant; but as he was the last of his profession in the whole district, they had elected him as a tourist attraction.

The siren sounded eerie in the *Höhenluft,* and the small group of people in the square listened to it glumly. When it was over, the loudspeaker of the Hotel Post blared out a sentimental song with the refrain *Auf Wiedersehen* to a busload of departing tourists. They were the last of the lot. The square suddenly felt empty. The villagers, accustomed to the despised crowd of strangers which normally filled it at this hour, felt left to themselves and did not like it.

Niko and Claire, out on a stroll, walked up to Gustav and inquired about the latest news on the radio. "Very bad news,"

Gustav said cheerfully. "The tourist season is *kaputt.*" In his privileged position he looked down with contempt at the bed-and-breakfast providers.

"And in Asia?" Claire asked.

Gustav shrugged. "Also very bad. They are shooting."

The Soloviefs installed themselves at a table on the empty terrace of the Hotel Post and ordered a bottle of wine and two pairs of *Würstl.* The mustard looked like liquid gold in the sun. It was the first time they were playing truant from a meal at the Kongresshaus.

"I won't try to cheer you up," said Claire. "This morning was a disaster."

"The conference is *kaputt,*" said Niko.

"There is still Tony and Valenti to come," said Claire. "And the general discussion."

"It will be the usual blindman's buff. What surprises me is that I don't care."

"I am all for not caring," said Claire, lifting her glass. "Here's to Burch's rats."

Suddenly they felt as if on a holiday. The natives called it *Galgenhumor.*

Tony's lecture, too, was a disappointment. His innocence, combined with impertinence, may have charmed Harriet and Blood, but did not go down well with most of the others.

Before he had even started to speak, Burch had raised his hand and demanded to be informed by Tony what his order —Burch confessed never to have heard of it—was "up to."

Tony was glad to comply. The Copertinian Order, he explained, derived its name from St. Joseph of Copertino, a wayward saint who lived in the seventeenth century and performed extraordinary feats of levitation at about the same time as Isaac Newton proclaimed the law of universal gravity. When his case for canonization came up before the Congregation of Rites, the part of the Devil's Advocate was played by Cardinal Lambertini, later Pope Benedict XIV, known as the Philosopher King. Lambertini was a notoriously sceptical expert on miracles, and looked with a jaundiced eye at the reports of Copertino's alleged aviatory achievements; but the eyewitness accounts finally convinced him, and it was Lambertini himself, when he became Pope, who published the decree of beatification. Among the many eyewitnesses were the Spanish ambassador to the Papal Court and his wife. When they passed through Assisi, where Copertino lived at the time, they expressed a desire to converse with him, and the Father Guardian sent word to his cell. But no sooner did the saint enter the church where the illustrious guests were assembled than his eyes became fixed on a statue of the Virgin standing in a niche high above the altar, and "he at once flew about a dozen paces above the heads of those present to the feet of the statue. After paying homage there for a short space and uttering his customary shrill cry, he flew back again to his cell, leaving the ambassador, his wife and the large retinue which attended them speechless with astonishment.

"And that," commented Tony, "might be called rather an understatement."

"Do you believe in that poppycock?" rasped Burch.

"I have been quoting the eyewitness accounts without drawing conclusions. We are held to that," Tony said smugly.

As for the activities of the order, he could only describe them in traditional terminology as being of a contemplative kind, making, however, extensive use of scientific method and electronic apparatus. These enabled the Brothers to take a shortcut to those substrata of the mind which otherwise are not easily attainable—"unless," Tony smiled engagingly, "you are willing to spend ten years in a Zen monastery or a Himalayan cave." It was common knowledge, he continued, that the conscious mind had little control over the emotions, and no awareness of the activities of its own nervous system. Several decades ago, a clumsy and unreliable gadget, vulgarly called a lie detector, provided a first step towards such an awareness. It recorded delicate changes in the electrical activity of the skin, induced by emotive reactions such as anger, fear and excitement, in response to certain words or situations —fleeting reactions of which the subject himself was unaware. Towards the end of the 1960s, new, more refined gadgets were invented, which enabled the user to be his own inquisitor and detect his own lies in the service of self-deception. These handy little machines transformed the changes in electric skin resistance into changes of pitch in a musical tone emitted by a loudspeaker. By listening to that tone, the subject obtained intimate information about the activities of his autonomic nervous system, and thus of the tensions and anxieties at the back of his mind. This information-feedback system, by making the person instantly aware of processes in the depths of the unconscious, at the same time enabled him to bring them to some extent under voluntary control. He could learn, in a short time, to relax his blood pressure, to alter his pulse rate, even his gastric secretion, and enter the contemplative state . . .

"Whatever that may mean," remarked Burch.

"It means," said John D. John, mollified by the term "feedback," "that mysticism can be cyberneticized."

"I would not talk of mysticism—not at this stage," said Tony. "It is merely the first step. But it shows that mind can perhaps one day gain complete control of the machine which is his body."

"Let's get to the next step," said Harriet, "without Cartesian speculations."

"You all know about it," said Tony, "but perhaps you regarded it as just another toy, while we have used it for our own devious purposes. So the next step was the control of our own brain waves. The new gadgets which came on the market in the early seventies enabled a person to be aware of the alpha waves which his brain emits. Among the various types of brain waves, the slow alpha rhythm, with frequencies around ten cycles per second, has long been known to be indicative of a state of mental relaxation. When the subject engages in intense mental activity such as an arithmetical calculation, the alpha rhythm is replaced by small, fast, irregular waves; when the problem is solved, it reappears. Yogis, Zen masters and other contemplatives have been found to produce a much higher than average amount of alpha waves. The new toys operate on the principle of the electroencephalograph with an added twist—they are tuned exclusively to alpha waves, which are heard as a series of bip-bips from a loudspeaker. After a few hours' training people can learn to increase their alpha activity . . ."

"And enter the contemplative state?" Burch quoted sarcastically.

"And enter the contemplative state," Tony repeated.

"Why not swallow some LSD and forget about the gadgets?"

"Because we are aiming in the opposite direction. We are not interested in taking trips."

"Then what are you interested in?"

"The sources of the Nile," Tony said amiably.

Blood chuckled. "Well roared," he said.

"Riddles are for kids," said Burch. "When are we getting to levitation?"

"So far we have only got to Omdurman," said Tony. "A kind of pseudolevitation, demonstrated in the late sixties by Dr. Valenti's colleague, Grey Walter, in Bristol. Two electrodes are attached to a young student's skull. In front of him is a television screen. When he presses a button, an exciting scene appears on it. Before he presses the button, his brain emits the characteristic 'intention wave,' a surge in electrical activity of some twenty microvolts. The electrodes transmit this wave to an amplifier, which activates a current, which switches on the exciting picture—a fraction of a second *before* the student has pressed the button. He soon discovers that there is no need to press the button at all—it is enough for him to *will* the picture, and it appears. Then he learns to switch *off* the picture by another act of will . . . I think this gets us a step further to the sources of the Nile. Walter reported that two of his adult experimental subjects became so excited by the discovery that they had the power to control the pictures on the screen by mere thinking and willing, that they wet their pants . . ."

Von Halder ruffled his mane to indicate protest, then lifted his hand. "So where does the magic come in? The electrodes are connected to the circuit, and it's all mechanical."

"Quite so," said Niko, "except for the act of willing, which produces the intention wave. From there on it's all mechanical. Before that it isn't."

"You see what I am driving at," said Tony. "You may regard the experiment as a stunt. Or as a metaphor. The wires deputize for the nerves, and the switch for the muscles, which in the normal course of events execute the act of will. But in the normal course of events we just take it for granted that the will can activate nerves and muscles, and thus we are unaware of the magic. Walter's mechanized metaphor drives it home. No wonder the subjects wet their pants. They are suddenly confronted with the naked mystery—the power of mind over matter."

"So I shall be impressed," said Halder, "when you will operate that television set without electrodes and wires on your skull."

"Something like that is indeed the next step in our little games," Tony said apologetically. "I should have explained that we do not regard contemplation as an end in itself. Rather we regard the contemplative state as the most favorable condition for our purpose, which is to tap the powers of mind at their source. We started where we think that Rhine and the bulk of researchers in parapsychology went wrong. They were leaning over backward to prove how modern and statistical their methods were, and became bogged down in dreary pedantry. They spent thousands of hours on rigorously controlled card-guessing and dice-throwing experiments—it's a miracle they did not die of boredom. Nevertheless, the odds against chance they produced were astronomical, and statistical evidence showed conclusively that telepathy and psychokinesis are facts, whether we like it or not . . ."

Burch shrugged expressively, while Halder threw his hands up to heaven. But Solovief intervened before the storm could break over Tony's head.

"I have seen the statistics," he said quietly, "and agree that they constitute *prima facie* evidence. I wouldn't mind the fact that they contradict the so-called laws of nature as we know them; Relativity and Quantum theory did the same—they contradicted the laws of nature as Newton knew them. But I do mind that the phenomena, though undeniably real, are so damned capricious and unpredictable."

"Hear, hear," said Halder.

"An experiment," said Burch, "which is not repeatable at will is not a scientific experiment."

"But Professor," Tony said, blushing, "if you were asked to make love to a beautiful lady on the village square with the whole fire brigade watching, the experiment would probably fail."

"You trying to be funny?" snapped Burch amidst suppressed giggles.

"I am trying to answer Professor Solovief's objection. The psi factor—or the sixth sense as it used to be called—must have its source in the deep substrata of the mind, beyond voluntary control—like sex. On this one issue even Freud and Jung agreed. The problem is to get down to that source. And that is where the relaxing apparatus and the alpha waves come in."

"And how far have you got?" asked Wyndham.

"We have got some pretty conclusive results," Tony said, smiling innocently.

"Conclusive of what?" Harriet wanted to know.

"Demonstrate them," said Burch. "Read my thoughts."

"That isn't difficult: 'Poppycock,' " said Tony.

There was some hilarity.

"Demonstrations are tricky," Tony continued. "Heisenberg's voodoo on physics, the indeterminacy principle, applies to our field too: the observer interacts with the observed phenomenon, and the situation becomes blurred. We have an old dear, Brother Jonas, who, when the spirit moves him and his alpha waves are right, can almost infallibly predict at which number the roulette ball will stop. Or perhaps he makes it stop at that number. He doesn't know and he doesn't care. But he couldn't do it in Monte Carlo—not yet. It's the fire brigade again."

"Forgive me," said Wyndham, "but if you are unable to demonstrate the results of your experiments, you cannot expect to convince people."

"Quite so. We do not expect it—not yet. For the time

being we are just playing games. Like the juggler of Notre Dame, who performed his tricks in the empty cathedral to make the Virgin on the altar smile."

"As a matter of fact," Niko said slowly, "I have seen some of the experiments of Tony's friends—in telepathy and also some physical phenomena—and I believe they have got something. This belief is shared by some of my hard-boiled colleagues, and also by some of Valenti's colleagues. Quite understandably, the order is afraid of premature publicity. Incidentally, they are also afraid of the military muscling in. You must be aware that both NASA and the Soviet Academy of Sciences are actively sponsoring research in these directions. And they usually know what they are up to."

"It just goes to show . . ." said Burch.

"To show what?" asked Blood.

"The power of ancient superstition."

"The most monumental superstition of our century," drawled Blood, "is the type of science which treats man as a salivating Pavlov dog, or an overgrown Skinner rat, or a Crick-robot programmed by its genetic code. Your science is a methodical form of paranoia."

"So what is your alternative?" shouted Halder. "Astrology, Maharishi, hippy-trippy, hash and mish-mash!"

"I have tried to explain," Tony said, "that we have to undergo a rather severe training to protect us against credulity and the contemporary variety of *nostalgie de la boue*—wallowing in muddy mysticism. We are not attracted by the fog, but by the light. By groping toward the light we are made to realize how deep the darkness is around us. We endeavor to make use of all that science can offer to get a glimpse at levels of reality which transcend science. The great scientists, from Pythagoras to Einstein, have always been aware of the fact—they even regarded it as a truism—that the scientific approach can only throw light on one limited aspect of reality, leaving the rest in darkness—as the human eye can only perceive a small fraction of the spectrum of radiations which surround and penetrate us . . ."

At this point, young Tony really got going. He compared the sneers which greeted the pioneers of psi-research with the hollow laughter that reverberated through the history of science whenever a heretic tried to break new ground. He got away with his impudent sermon because he was surprisingly well grounded in the history of science—of which most scientists have only a foggy idea. He pointed out that, contrary to common belief, Canon Copernicus throughout his lifetime had been a darling of the Catholic clergy, but mortally afraid of his academic colleagues; that Galileo had been an intimate buddy of Pope Urban VIII—until he started meddling with theology—but was persecuted by the scientific establishment of his time; and that when Kepler suggested that the tides were caused by the attraction of the moon, the same enlightened Galileo dismissed the idea as an occult fancy. And so on, through Harvey, Pasteur, Planck and Einstein . . .

"All right, all right," Halder broke in. "So the genius, the pioneer, always has a tough time. But there always are a million cranks to one genius."

"Quite so," said Tony. "But unfortunately, only posterity can tell whether the poor chap was a genius or a crank."

"And sometimes he is both," Wyndham giggled. "Even, with due respect, our dear Nikolai seems today to be inclined . . ."

"Your dear Nikolai," Solovief said, unsmiling, "is not a Galileo, but he knows at least as much about physics as any undergraduate. And any hopeful undergrad will tell you that the motto of modern physics is, to quote the great Niels Bohr, 'the madder the better.' I admit that some of the notions suggested by Tony's psi factor make one's hair stand on end. But they sound a little less preposterous in the light of the equally wild concepts of subatomic physics. Let me remind you, once more, that *we* don't turn a hair at the notion that an electron can be in two places at once, that it can race for a while backward in time, that space has holes in it, that mass can be negative and that the materialist's matter ultimately consists of vibrations emitted by nonexistent strings. I am sometimes tempted to take at face value Eddington's epigram that the stuff of the world is mind stuff; or Jean's offhand remark that the universe looks more like a thought than a machine. So why should your hair react differently when you listen to Tony and when you listen to me?"

"You are a loss to poetry," said Blood.

"Forgive my stubbornness," Wyndham piped up, "but even if you succeeded in convincing me that these puzzling phenomena are real, I can't for the life of me see their relevance to the strategy of survival, or the message that is supposed to emanate from this conference."

Tony looked questioningly at Niko, who merely shrugged his massive shoulders. So Tony had to soldier on. "I haven't got even the beginnings of a precise answer to your precise question," he said. "Assuming, hopefully, that we should succeed in stabilizing the phenomena and getting them under conscious control—the outcome of such a breakthrough would still be quite unpredictable. Instead of an answer, I can offer you only an analogy. The Greeks knew that when they rubbed a piece of *elektron,* that is, amber, with a silk cloth, it acquired the curious virtue of attracting flimsy objects. But they regarded this as a freak phenomenon which could not be fitted into the frame of orthodox Aristotelian physics and was therefore unworthy of attention. For the next two thousand years electricity was ignored. Only in the late eighteenth century did it gain admission into respectable scientific laboratories, and this eventually led to a revolution which transformed the world. But nobody at the time could have foreseen to what consequences it would lead. If Dr. Wyndham's question had been put to Galvani or Volta, they would have been at a loss for an answer, and would probably have said that they were just playing games with frogs' legs and Leyden jars. Not in their wildest dreams could it have occurred to them that the freak phenomenon they were investigating would turn out to be the ultimate constituents of matter, and the source of all power and light . . ."

"So you are dreaming, young man, that this psi factor will change the world and reveal the secret of the universe?" Halder's hair seemed to bristle with static electricity.

"Dreams," Tony said coyly, "are private property. However," he continued, "one cannot a priori rule out the possibility that we live submerged in an ocean of psi forces—a sort of psycho-magnetic field—of which we are unaware, as we are unaware of electric fields. When we have come to grips with it, this might lead to a new Copernican revolution. It may not change the world, but it may change our outlook on the world. I thought you agreed that such a change was our most urgent need."

"Do you mean," asked John D. John, "that it might lead to the up-opening of new systems of communication channels? From the point of view of information theory this may be a welcome project so long as it is not counterproductive."

"Amen," said Tony. "If you wish to put it that way."

"I would rather put it this way," said Solovief. "Our main trouble is that we no longer have a coherent world view—neither the theologian nor the physicist. God is dead, but materialism is also dead, since matter has become a meaningless word. Causality, determinism, the clockwork universe of Newton, have been buried without ceremony. Tony's friends may be crazy, and that is why they appeal to me. Perhaps that alpha-wave machine will turn out to be the new Leyden jar."

"So do you suggest," Harriet said dryly, "that we ask Congress for a research allocation to discover whether that saint, whose name I cannot remember, did indeed levitate over the head of the Spanish ambassador?"

In view of her known devotion to Niko, Harriet's sarcasm was the more effective—and wounding; it expressed the general dismay of the assembly at the revelation of Niko's unexpected cranky side.

"That would not be a bad idea," Niko said calmly. "Particularly since, as I said, the military seem to have already cottoned on to the idea. Now I think it is time for cocktails."

The meeting broke up in general embarrassment, as if they had been shown a very dirty film.

Bruno Kaletski had been recalled to Washington.

He had been absent from Tony's lecture, and had spent most of the afternoon in the glass telephone cage of the Kongresshaus, waiting for calls which never got through, or if they did, were cut off instantly by exchange Fräuleins on the verge of nervous breakdowns. He did, however, put in a hurried appearance at the cocktail party to say his farewells before Gustav drove him down to the valley, where he was to take the night train to the nearest airport. He managed to shake hands with everybody, two people at a time, not omitting the staff, his arms crossed as if dancing a quadrille, yet without dropping the bulky briefcase under his elbow. Then he was gone—a small, bustling figure, touching in his naïve self-importance, exasperating and disarming at the same time.

All other American participants had received telegrams from their consulate advising them not to prolong unduly their sojourn abroad in view of the international situation, and of possible dislocations in transport. Through the plate-glass windows the village looked dark and deserted; now that the tourists were gone, the natives were economizing on electricity. The Kongresshaus stood out under the stars, a blazing, lonely lighthouse.

The Call Girls milled around a little sheepishly in the cocktail room, waiting for the gloom to lift with the second or third martini. A few—mainly staff—were listening to the news on the radio, but most of them did not bother. The Soloviefs stood by themselves in a corner. They were, for once, left alone, as nobody was anxious to continue the discussion about Tony's hare-brained order, or Niko's defection and flight into the occult darkness.

"Do you think this time it's *really* serious?" asked Claire.

Solovief shrugged expressively. "I put the same silly question to Bruno before he left. Do you know what his answer was? He grabbed my arm just above the elbow—he always does that; gripped hard, looked deep into my eyes, and said: *'It all depends*—I can say no more.' " Solovief took a fresh glass of martini from the tray that Hansie offered, without emptying the previous one.

"Have I ever asked you," asked Claire, "whether you take Bruno seriously?"

Niko made a grimace. *"It all depends,"* he said. "They have in these parts a national hero—*der kleine Moritz,* a sort of counterpart to Alice, but a more cynical little brat. And they have a saying: History is made just as *der kleine Moritz* imagines it."

"Then what *is* serious?"

"Don't you know? A toothache is serious. When it is really bad you forget to worry about the future of mankind. But it does not work the other way round."

"Then I am all for toothaches. Have you got one?"

There were times when he had to be treated like a child, and they both played their roles as best they could.

By dinner time spirits had risen again. Gustav had arranged with the proprietor of the Hotel Post, now without a single customer, for a folkloristic cabaret show to be put on specially for the Call Girls. It was all very jolly; the fire brigade did their best with yodeling and mutual arse-slapping; at one stage von Halder joined in and earned enthusiastic applause. His stomping and sweating had an almost professional touch; he was taking it really seriously.

Friday

The last morning session of the Symposium was devoted to Dr. Cesare Valenti's presentation. It was expected to provide some dramatic entertainment, and it did.

He had the self-confidence characteristic of famous surgeons, and he was also an accomplished showman. His manner was both self-assured and reassuring to patients; and his cheerfully encouraging smile made everyone feel like a patient.

Valenti started by paying a handsome compliment to Tony, whose command of such recondite matters as alpha rhythms and intention waves had seemed to him, Valenti, most remarkable. He was in full sympathy with Tony's line of research which, if he understood rightly, aimed at the attainment of levels of consciousness or states of mind far superior to the humdrum routines of everyday existence. His own work as a neurosurgeon had a more modest aim: to restore patients suffering from some disorder of mind or brain to just that normal, humdrum routine. He wished to confess, however, from the start, his strong suspicion that a certain type of mental disorder was endemic in the human species; and that if some form of mass therapy was not discovered fairly soon, the said species would come to an end. But he wished to demonstrate first some recent advances in methods of individual therapy, "and to discuss the problem of mankind at large at the end of my chatter." (Valenti's English was as carefully polished as were his fingernails, but it retained some minute rugosities, such as the failure to distinguish between "talk," "chat" and "chatter.")

"To begin with, I shall show you a film of a very strange bullfight, although some of you may have seen it already. It was made by my eminent colleague Dr. José Delgado of Yale University in the middle nineteen-sixties. The animal you will see is a so-called brave bull, a race specially bred for its ferociousness. Unlike a tame bull, which reacts indifferently to human beings, a brave bull will launch a deadly attack at first sight of a person. As you will presently see . . ."

Valenti made a graceful sign to the ubiquitous Gustav, who had been waiting at the back of the room. He deftly let down the projection screen, activated the automatic window blinds and set the projector whirring. An empty bullring appeared, basking in the sun, with no spectators or fighters in view. Then a lonely man entered the ring, dressed in jeans and a polo-neck sweater. Instead of a weapon, he carried a small instrument which looked like a portable radio set with a rod antenna. Next, a very nasty-looking bull was let into the arena. No sooner had it caught sight of the Professor than it started trotting towards him, then broke into its characteristic express-train charge. When the bull was but a few yards away and it seemed that the Professor could only be saved by a miracle, the miracle materialized. The camera showed in close-up the Professor's fingers nimbly turning a switch on his radio. Its horns now only a few inches from the Professor's abdomen, the bull came to an abrupt halt, as if he had hit an invisible wall, then slowly turned away, as if thoroughly bored. The Professor activated another switch and the bull went "moo." This action was repeated ten times and each time it went "moo." The bull had become as meek as a lamb.

Valenti signaled to Gustav, the window blinds went up as if by another act of magic, the mountain panorama returned to its rightful place, and Valenti continued his lecture:

"You have seen one of the many applications of the technique known as electrical stimulation of the brain, or ESB for short. The bull has several electrodes—thin platinum needles—permanently implanted at various depths in specific areas of its brain. The electrodes are connected to a microminiaturized radio transmitter/receiver—a 'stimoceiver'—fixed with dental cement to the animal's skull. This apparatus enables the experimenter to receive information about activities in the animal's brain, but also to stimulate activity in any chosen area by minute electric impulses controlled by radio. In the little drama that you have just seen, Professor Delgado brought the bull to a sudden stop, then made it turn to one side, by activating electrodes in the motor cortex on the roof of the brain, and at the same time stimulating those centers deep down in the midbrain which inhibit aggressive emotions. He was able to control not only the bull's movements, but also to change abruptly its mood from violence to docility . . ."

Over the last decade, Valenti continued, electrical stimulation of the brain by radio-controlled, implanted electrodes had been applied to rats, cats, monkeys, dolphins, crickets and bulls. It was found possible by this method to control the animal's movements and postures; to evoke rage, fear and docility; amorous and maternal comportment or its opposite. Gustav was called into action once more as Valenti demonstrated in a series of brief scenes what the sagacious electrodes could do. Playful cats were suddenly turned into savage tigers by stimulating their lateral hypothalamus, and just as suddenly became purring pets again. A monkey was shown gobbling a banana with evident relish. When it was halfway through it, the experimenter was seen pressing a button. The monkey instantly stopped chewing, took the banana out of its mouth and threw it away. Valenti commented: "This time the impulse acted on the caudate nucleus," and he pointed with his stick at an anatomical chart on the wall, where that small nucleus appeared like an orange pip deeply embedded in the pulp. Then a cat was shown lapping milk and suddenly stopping, its tongue hanging out, all motion frozen in the position in which the animal had been caught by the current. Monkeys were shown who, though previously indifferent to female advances, were turned into sex maniacs of athletic prowess. Lively chimpanzees were made to fall asleep within thirty seconds through stimulation of the septal area. Female rhesus monkeys, who spend most of their time affectionately nursing and grooming their babies, were made to lose all interest in them and reject their pitiful approaches, so that they had to take refuge with some other mother; inhibition of the maternal instinct lasted for about ten minutes after each midbrain stimulation.

The last film was a hilarious sequence preceded by the title THE TAMING OF A DICTATOR. The dictator in question was an ill-tempered creature called Nero, undisputed boss of a colony of about a dozen monkeys living in a large cage. Half of the cage was Nero's personal territory which no lesser mortal was allowed to enter—the others had to live crowded together in the farthest corner of the cage. The boss also enjoyed the customary privileges of precedence in matters of sex and food. His authority was maintained by making threatening gestures and sounds at any sign of insubordination; even glaring at the culprit was often sufficient to terrorize him, while his subjects dared only to steal furtive glances at the boss.

Came the day when Nero was taken out of the cage, given an anesthetic, and electrodes were implanted. When he woke up, all he knew was that a little box had grown out of his skull like a bump which could not be removed, and to which he soon became accustomed; the electrodes in the brain do not make their presence directly felt. But within a single hour from the start of their activation Nero was forced to abdicate his rule. Radiostimulation of the caudate nucleus was applied for five seconds per minute. With each stimulation Nero's facial expression became more peaceful and benign, the threatening gestures and glances vanished, the growls ceased—and his subjects were quick to read the signs. Within that hour they lost their fear of the boss, invaded his territory and crowded him without any sign of respect.

It seemed too good to be true. It was. "This, my friends, is only the first act of the drama," Valenti commented. "Now watch Act Two."

It was short and sad. The radio signals to Nero's caudate nucleus were stopped. Within ten minutes he was the boss again. As minute after minute passed and the electrodes remained inactive, Nero's ferocious glares, the baring of teeth and pawing of the floor reappeared; as a result, the citizens of the short-lived democracy resumed their cringing and retreated to their safe corner.

"But now," Valenti announced, "watch for Act Three. It is the best of all."

Though the apparent transformation of Nero's character had been gradual, the most dramatic changes in his behavior had occurred during the critical five-second periods of actual stimulation, at intervals of a minute. While the electrostimulation lasted, he looked like a yogi in samadhi. After Nero's return to power, the experimenter played a new trick on him. He installed, in a conspicuous position inside the cage, a lever. When the lever was pressed down, it automatically triggered off a five-second activation of the electrodes in Nero's brain, and made him temporarily docile again. One clever monkey—a female called Dolores—soon discovered that pressing the lever had this wonderful effect on the boss. Whenever Nero threatened her, she pressed the lever, instantly inhibiting his aggressive demeanor. She even got into the habit of staring straight into Nero's eyes—which before the advent of the lever had been considered as *lèse majesté*. Nero remained Boss, but he was no longer the absolute ruler, for Dolores learned not only to block his attacks directed against herself but also against others, and to press the lever whenever Nero became ill-tempered.

"And so," Valenti concluded, "that little colony of monkeys lived happily ever after. And here ends *my* little parable, to use Dr. Caspari's expression. But it is time now to proceed from animals to humans. In a few minutes I shall have the pleasure of giving you a live experimental demonstration of radio-controlled behavior in a human being. But first I must go through the routine of the usual reassurances—like the air hostess putting the safety belt on—though in this illustrious company there is hardly any need for it . . ."

Valenti proceeded to explain, in a slightly bored voice, that the implanting of electrodes into human brains was, of course, only done for therapeutic purposes; the new scientific insights gained by applying the method were a welcome bonus, nothing more. Thousands of patients all over the world were going about their business with twenty to forty electrodes permanently anchored in their brains. They were implanted under local anesthesia and could remain in place for years, without causing any discomfort. The brain is insensitive to touch, it can be cut, frozen, cauterized, without the patient being aware of it; it is so well protected inside the skull that it needs no sensory or pain receptors. Neurosurgeons have for a long time been in the habit of operating on conscious patients who keep chattering with the doctor and feel no pain while the affected parts of their brain are excised. But the earlier methods of lobotomy, leucotomy or electro-shock therapy were sheer butchery compared with the use of the delicate electrode needles. They were connected to sockets cemented to the patient's skull, which could be hidden by a bandage, or a wig, or some elaborate coiffure. The disorders thus treated included epilepsy, intractable pain, insomnia, severe anxiety and depression, uncontrollable violence and some forms of schizophrenia. Some cases were treated in outpatients' departments where they received electric brain stimulation at regular intervals; others carried in their pockets portable stimulators which enabled them to activate the electrodes when they felt an attack of pain or of violent rage coming on. Needles implanted in the so-called pleasure centers of the hypothalamus gave patients a feeling of euphoria or of erotic arousal which sometimes ended in the psychic equivalent of an orgasm.

"Does that also serve a therapeutic purpose?" grunted Blood.

"It may, in certain cases," Valenti said cautiously, realizing that he had gone too far in alluding to certain rather esoteric lines of research.

"What's wrong with good old mas-tur-bation?" Blood wanted to know. "You don't need platinum needles for that."

Valenti's smile became even more polite, but he ignored Blood. "There have also been successful experiments in which we use the electrodes to establish two-way radio communication between the subject's brain and a computer. The computer is programmed to recognize disturbances in the electrical activity of the brain which signal the approach of an epileptic attack or a fit of violent rage; when the computer is thus alerted, it activates by radio the needles in the inhibitory centers which block the attack . . . And now, I think, I have given you the necessary information, and we can proceed with the demonstration." He signaled to Gustav. "Call Miss Carey, please."

Most of the participants had paid no attention to the fact —or had not even noticed it—that Miss Carey was absent from the session, and the tape recorder was operated by Claire.

"Miss Carey," Valenti explained while they were waiting for her to appear, "was sent to me as a patient with severe anxiety alternating with violent episodes in which she attacked members of her family, particularly her younger, married sister . . ."

There was an uneasy silence while they waited, as in a dentist's waiting room with its collective awareness of the unpleasant experience ahead. At last the glass swing door was flung open with a flourish by Gustav, who held it courteously for Miss Carey to pass. She was smiling, and fingering the gray bun on top of her head. All glances were momentarily on that bun, then hurriedly lowered to dossiers and writing pads.

"Good morning, Miss Carey," Valenti smiled. "Will you please sit over there?"

He indicated a chair which stood isolated in a corner of the room, placed there at his request before the beginning of the session. Miss Carey sat down primly, apparently enjoying the occasion. Half the participants had to turn their chairs round.

"Now, Miss Carey," Valenti addressed her, adjusting his wristwatch, which was of an unusually large size, "you don't mind taking part in this little demonstration?"

"Love it," Miss Carey replied. "Anything you say, Doctor."

"Before you came to the clinic, you were not too well?"

"I was terrible," said Miss Carey.

"What was troubling you?"

"All sorts of foolish things."

"Won't you tell us about it?"

"I was a silly girl," Miss Carey giggled.

"What were you afraid of?"

"I don't like to remember. Just silly things."

"But you must tell us. You are all right now, and you know that by cooperating in these demonstrations you are helping other patients to recover."

Miss Carey nodded, still giggling. "I know, Doctor, but I just don't like to remember."

"Shall I help you to remember?" He again adjusted some dial on his complicated wristwatch. "Now, Eleanor. Tell us what it felt like to be frightened."

A ghastly change took place in Miss Carey. Her face went ashen, her breath became labored as if she had an attack of asthma, her spindly fingers gripped the armrests of the chair as if sitting in an airplane that was going to crash.

"Don't do that," she panted. "Please stop it."

"What are you frightened of?"

"I don't know. I feel that something dreadful is going to happen." She was twisting and turning in her chair, exploring the corner of the room behind her back. "I feel that a man is standing behind me."

"There is only the wall."

"I know but I feel it. Please stop it, stop. For the love of Christ."

"You were also frightened of being sent to hell for your sins. But you know there is no hell."

"How do you know? I have seen those pictures." A tremor ran through her body and did not stop.

"What pictures?"

"Stop it . . ." Suddenly she screamed. Blood got up noisily and shambled out of the room. Miss Carey screamed a second time and seemed on the verge of hysterics. Valenti adjusted his dials. Her body suddenly relaxed, she took several deep breaths and her color returned.

"There you are, Eleanor," Valenti said. "All is well again."

She nodded. Both were smiling.

"Do you mind having gone through the experiment?"

"Not in the least, Doctor, I was just being silly again."

"Do you have any hostile feelings towards me?"

Miss Carey shook her head vigorously. She was becoming increasingly animated. "I would like to kiss your hands, Doctor," she giggled. "You are my savior."

She watched him adjusting a dial. "Ah," she sighed. "This feels lovely. It must be the naughty needle. Naughty, naughty. You are doing it . . ."

Her expression became ecstatic. Suddenly Harriet shouted, "Rot. Stop it. This is an obscenity."

Solovief rapped the table. "I think you have made your point, Dr. Valenti."

But already Miss Carey had returned to normal. Doctor and patient were again smiling at each other. "Some of these gentlemen—and ladies—seemed to be upset," Valenti said to her. "Do you understand why they were upset, Miss Carey?"

She shook her head, her wrinkled face resuming its look of the benevolent, aging nun. "No, Doctor, I just noticed Sir Evelyn leaving the room."

Valenti bowed to her politely. "Thank you very much, Miss Carey. Well, ladies and gentlemen, this is the end of the demonstration. As you may have noticed, our electronic wizards have succeeded in reducing the radiostimulator to the size of a wristwatch." He put the gadget down on the table. "If anybody is interested, I shall be glad to explain the mechanism. And now, to bring my chatter to an end, we may perhaps draw certain conclusions from these studies, which apply not only to individual patients, but to mankind as a whole . . ."

But after the demonstration with Miss Carey, Valenti's diagnosis of the human condition met with a certain resistance, if not hostility. He pointed out that Miss Carey had evidently been conscious of her experiences under electrical stimulation, and remembered them afterwards, but was not in the least upset by the memory. She remembered her *thoughts,* but this did not revive the *emotions* which had accompanied them. Similarly, those ideas—like eternal damnation—which had frightened the wits out of her at the time of her illness, now that she was cured, appeared to her merely as "all sorts of foolish notions." But even now, after her cure, those attacks of ghastly fear could still be evoked by stimulation of the deep, archaic structures of the brain in which they originated. Similarly, feelings of elation or love and devotion could be elicited from other areas of that ancient and primitive part of the brain which man had in common with his animal ancestors—the seat of instincts, passions and biological drives. These antediluvian structures at the very core of the brain had hardly been touched by the nimble fingers of evolution. In contrast to this anachronistic core, the modern structures of the human brain—the rind or neocortex—had expanded during the last half a million years at a truly explosive speed which was without precedent in the whole history of evolution; so much so that some older anatomists compared it to a tumorous growth. But explosions tend to upset the balance of nature, and the brain explosion in the middle of the Pleistocene gave birth to a mentally unbalanced species. If anybody were to doubt this statement, he only had to look at human history through the eyes of a dispassionate zoologist from another planet. The disastrous historical record pointed to a biological malfunction; more precisely, it indicated that those recently evolved structures of the brain, which endowed man with language and logic, had never become properly integrated with, and coordinated with, the ancient, emotionbound structures on which they were superimposed during their explosive proliferation. Owing to this evolutionary blunder, old brain and new brain, emotion and reason, when not in acute conflict, lead an agonized co-existence. On one side, the pale cast of rational thought, of logic suspended on a thin thread all too easily broken; on the other, the native fury of passionately held irrational beliefs—which, as Dr. Epsom had pointed out, were responsible for the holocausts of past and present history. The neocortex had been compared to a computer; but when a computer was fed biased data, the outcome was bound to be disastrous . . .

"My good man," interrupted Blood, who had shambled back to his seat after the demonstration, "there is nothing new in this. I can quote you a hundred sonorous passages written by the best professional diagnosticians—the poets—who assure us that man is mad, and always has been."

"But if you will forgive me," Valenti smiled, "poets are not taken seriously, and never have been. Today, however, we possess the evidence, from anatomy, psychology and brain research, that our species, as a whole, is afflicted by a paranoid streak, not in the metaphysical but in the clinical sense; and that this condition, by an evolutionary mistake, is built into our brains. My eminent colleague, Dr. Paul MacLean, has coined the term *schizophysiology* for this condition; he defines it, if I may quote him, as a 'dichotomy in the functions of the phylogenetically old and new cortex that might account for differences between emotional and intellectual behavior. While our intellectual functions are carried out in the newest and most highly developed part in the brain, our emotive behavior continues to be dominated by a relatively crude and primitive system, by archaic structures in the brain whose fundamental pattern has undergone hardly any change in the whole course of evolution from rat to man . . .'

"And this brings me to the conclusion of my chatter. Evolution has made many mistakes; the fossil record shows that to each surviving species there are hundreds that perished. Turtles are beautiful animals, but they are so top-heavy that if by misadventure they fall on their backs, they cannot get up again. Many elegant insects are victims of the same engineering mistake. If evolution is under divine guidance, then the dear Lord must be very fond of experimenting. If it is a natural process, then it must proceed by trial and error. But man, although mad, has engaged in a dialogue with God; he has acquired the power to transcend biological frontiers and correct the shortcomings and errors in his native equipment. The first step, however, is a correct diagnosis. This, I believe, dear friends, modern brain research can provide. If our diagnosis is correct, the therapy will follow. We already have the power to cure individual patients—who are the extreme examples of the collective disorder which afflicts our species. Soon we shall have the power to attack it at its roots, and produce an artificial mutation by neuroengineering. As I have said before, a desperate situation needs desperate remedies. And to quote another of my eminent colleagues, Professor Moyne: 'It appears that the scientists in brain research stand on a threshold similar to the one on which atomic physicists stood in the early 1940s.' This is the end of my chatter."

Like the other Call Girls, Valenti had started haltingly, with well-worn clichés and oratorial tricks, but had gradually warmed to his subject and ended on a note of sincerity, even passion. But was not that passion, too, inspired by the archaic structures deep down in the spongy tissues of his brain; and were the data presented to the computer perhaps also biased by them?

The discussion after Valenti's paper was chaotic, as usual, but ended in an unusually dramatic fashion. Von Halder spoke first, repeating what he had said before: aggression was endemic in *Homo homicidus;* individual therapy—however clever the methods of Valenti and his colleagues—was not enough; the urgent need was for M.A.T.—Mass Abreaction Therapy—organized on an international scale.

Harriet wanted to know whether Valenti's needles were able to block not only aggression but also misguided devotion—to immunize against morbid infatuation with a Circe or a Duce.

John D. John, Jr., objected to the comparison of the neocortex with a computer that was fed biased data. From the cybernetician's point of view the whole of the nervous system was a computer which could not be programmed to mislead itself, otherwise it would go haywire.

"Perhaps it does," giggled Wyndham.

"That is not the communication theorist's view," John D., Jr., replied dryly.

Burch objected to the distinction Valenti had made between so-called reason and so-called emotion, and his references to a so-called mind, that hypothetical ghost in the machine which nobody had ever seen. All these terms belonged to the vocabulary of an outmoded psychology; modern science considered only the measurable data of observable behavior as legitimate subjects of study, providing the basis for social engineering.

When it was Petitjacques's turn to speak, he produced with a flourish a roll of Scotch tape and stuck it across his lips. Nobody could make out what the gesture was meant to symbolize, and it failed to impress. Tempers were getting rather frayed; it was past lunch time. Halder seemed particularly irritable; his gastric juices turned nasty when a meal was delayed.

Wyndham confessed to having been profoundly impressed by Valenti's demonstration, but he wondered whether it really pointed in the right direction for a possible therapy. He could not help still believing that the future of our species would be decided by what he had called "the battle of the womb," and "the revolution in the cradle"; and thus ultimately by certain new methods of education to which he had referred in his paper . . .

Tony apologized for feeling impelled to make a frivolous remark. The Middle Ages had made a sharp, and perhaps wise, distinction between white and black magic. It had struck him at certain moments on that morning that the same distinction could possibly be made between the experiments he had referred to in his own talk, and those shown in Dr. Valenti's somewhat terrifying demonstrations.

Miss Carey, in her chair, was becoming increasingly fidgety as one critical speech followed the other. Her rather fixed stare, however, was directed not at the actual speaker but at Claire, who was usurping Miss Carey's rightful place at the tape recorder. Claire noticed the stare and tried a sympathetic smile, which made no impression. On the contrary, that hypocritical smile reminded Miss Carey even more of her married sister. For a while she fingered the bun on her head, then she produced a half-finished pullover of hideous colors from her bag and busied herself with knitting.

Valenti's reply to the discussion was brief, delivered in a somewhat strained voice. Owing to the late hour, he explained, he had to concentrate on what seemed to him the most relevant points. He felt confident that neurophysiology would soon find the answer—if it had not already been found by one of the many research teams working in that field—to inhibit not only aggressive impulses, but also what Dr. Epsom had called morbid infatuation—whether with a person, a totem or a dogma. As for von Halder's objection, he wholeheartedly agreed that individual therapy was not enough. But he begged to disagree with Halder's whole concept of abreaction therapy. The methods von Halder proposed, instead of inhibiting aggression, were designed to enhance it. His own methods, and those of his colleagues, aimed in the opposite direction: to enhance the inhibitory control which the new brain exercised over the archaic structures of the old one. This could be done, and was being done, in both animal and man. But it was only the beginning. Science had only just started exploring and mapping that unknown continent, the brain. As our knowledge of it increased, and the maps became more precise, so would our methods of physiological control. We had progressed from the surgeon's knife to the radio-controlled electrode. The next step would perhaps lead from electrical to biochemical controls. Certain aggression centers, and aggression-blocking centers in the brain were sensitive to particular hormone balances. Already in the 1960s it was shown that the savage rhesus monkey could be readily turned into a friendly animal by the administration of Librium—not sedated, but tamed. Other preparations had a comparable effect on violent psychotics. He paused, then continued slowly in a voice which he tried to make sound casual: "It is not unlikely that in a few years, and after a few more wars and massacres, it will be realized that the only salvation for our species is to put specific anti-hostility agents into the water supply, in addition to chlorine and other approved anti-pollutants. Needless to say . . ."

Valenti had almost finished when Halder made the mistake of interrupting him, though he could not have foreseen the ghastly consequences. Ruffling his white mane with the familiar King Lear gesture, he shouted, pointing at Miss Carey in her chair, *"Ach so!* First you turn this poor lady's brain into a pincushion, and now you want to turn us into zombies. I will not . . ."

But nobody was to know the end of the sentence. This was altogether too much for Miss Carey. She had been the center of attention and then forgotten in her chair. All those horrid people were criticizing and attacking her doctor instead of kissing the savior's hands. The reference to pincushions and zombies was the last straw. Miss Carey jumped out of her chair, improbably brandishing her knitting needle. With her other hand she grabbed the wristwatch which the doctor had left on the conference table after the demonstration. Thus armed, she lunged not at Halder, but at innocent Claire, who so much reminded her of her sister, queening it at the tape recorder.

The whole action went off so fast that afterwards everybody remembered a different version of it. There was an ugly mess on Claire's arm where the knitting needle had gone in and been torn out again, but she had not uttered a sound. Miss Carey herself, struggling and screaming, was effectively restrained by the athletic Halder, who had been the first to get at her, and to pin her elbows behind her back; while Valenti, white-faced, forced open her fists to retrieve the needle and watch. But that delicate gadget, submitted to such brutal treatment, had lost its magic. Miss Carey had to be half dragged, half carried to her room, uttering vile words of protest and intermittent shrieks, until Valenti, after another painful struggle, managed to put her to sleep with an injection. The proceedings were watched wide-eyed by Hansie and Mitzie, the impassive Gustav, and by three members of the voluntary fire brigade who had been drinking beer in the Kongresshaus kitchen. However, by the time the ambulance arrived from the valley there was no need for it, as Miss Carey was fast asleep, smiling like the saintly nun she would no doubt have become but for some schizophysiological malformation in her caudate nucleus.

After a hurried lunch of soup grown cold under a greasy film, of goulash that had disintegrated in the oven, and fruit salad out of tins from the American army surplus, the Call

Girls assembled once more in the conference room for the closing session. According to the agenda, it was to be devoted to the summing up by Professor Solovief, followed by the General Discussion, and the drafting of the Resolution or Message. Niko's idea of an "action committee" had been quietly dropped somewhere along the line.

They were in a chastened, almost solemn mood—a gang of rowdies attending Sunday school. All had their dossiers, pads and pencils neatly laid out in front of them on the table of polished pine. Claire, earphones over her smooth chestnut hair, was again in charge of the tape recorder. She had a neat bandage over her arm, and had been given a shot of penicillin in spite of her protest against the unnecessary fuss—in fact she was quite glad about it, as the idea of having any trace of Miss Carey's knitting needle in her blood filled her with an irrational horror. Miss Carey herself was still under sedation in her room.

Before Solovief could start on his summary, Valenti got up and made a handsome apology to all those who had witnessed that painful scene, and in particular "to our charming hostess, who was in danger of becoming a martyr to science." The joke did not go down very well. He had regained his composure, but they had all noticed during the morning session the brittleness of his elegant façade, the hairline cracks in his self-assurance. He took full responsibility for the incident, explaining that for the last two years Miss Carey had been under complete control, and had participated in a number of similar demonstrations without a single hitch. The morning's incident had been due to a minute fault in the apparatus which, fortunately, had now been put right. He concluded with his repeated apologies, and the rather unnecessary request that everybody should be nice to Miss Carey when she emerged from her slumbers, and act as if nothing had happened. She herself would in all probability regard the incident as just a bit of "silly behavior"—and feel no emotion nor remorse.

Valenti's statement was received in silence. Solovief thanked him rather dryly and immediately launched into the onerous task of summing up the proceedings of the conference.

He reminded his listeners of his opening address in which he had set out some of the considerations—known to them all—which made the survival of *Homo sapiens* a questionable proposition. In those opening remarks he had suggested that the task of the conference should be to inquire into the causes of man's predicament, to formulate a tentative diagnosis, and to suggest possible remedies.

As regards the first point, several causative factors had been suggested by various participants, which might complement each other, but as yet hardly provided a coherent synthesis. Thus, for instance, Dr. Wyndham had hinted at the possibility that man's troubles began with the prenatal squeeze on the embryo in the womb, the trauma of a clumsily laborious birth, and, above all, the protracted helplessness and suggestibility of the human infant. Another theory put the blame on the dramatic increase of mutual dependence and tribal solidarity during the critical period when man's hominid ancestors emerged from the forests onto the plains and—in a first outburst of *hubris*—took to hunting prey faster and stronger than themselves. Both factors taken together may have molded man into the worshipful, frightened and fanatical creature that he became. Other primate societies were also held together by social forces, but the family bonds did not grow into neurotic attachments; the cohesive forces within the group did not attain the intensity and fervor of tribal feelings; and occasional tensions between groups did not result in war and genocide. As Dr. Epsom had pointed out, these fratricidal tendencies were enhanced, instead of being diminished, by the acquisition of language, with its power to erect intra-specific barriers, to promote dogmatic belief and formulate explosive battle slogans. A fourth factor was the simultaneous acceptance of death by the intellect, and its rejection by instinct, which implanted the sinister double helix of anxiety and guilt into the collective mind. Lastly, Dr. Valenti had attempted to define the physiological malfunction underlying the paranoid streak reflected in man's history—the chronic conflict between emotion and reason, instinct and intelligence; the compulsion to live, die and kill for irrational beliefs which were unaffected by logic, and overrode the instinct of self-preservation.

Niko paused. He kept glancing sideways at Claire, worried about the possibility of an infection. She on her side was achingly aware of how tired he looked. He kept clearing his throat, which was not his habit.

"So much, then," he continued, "for the pathogenic factors which seem to have made us into what we are. I realize that I have left out much of what was said on this subject —but we have the tape recordings which will put that right in the printed version of the proceedings."

This was no doubt correct; but it did not prevent several participants—Halder and Burch in particular—from resenting not having been so far mentioned by name. The main function of a chairman winding up a symposium is to hand out chocolates.

But Niko would have none of it. If this was a circus, he was still the ringmaster. He had to make a last effort, and try to make them face up to their responsibilities. He lowered his head, recovering his former bellicosity, and his voice regained its resonance.

He declared himself in essential agreement with the view that man was an evolutionary misfit—a glorious freak who built cathedrals and composed symphonies, but still a freak, with built-in compulsions which drove him towards ultimate self-destruction. Von Halder had reminded them that social animals fought harmless duels for mating partners and territorial possession; man did the reverse—he fought for mirages with liquid phosphorous, fought for slogans with nuclear bombs.

Dr. Kaletski had repeatedly warned the conference against taking a catastrophic view of recent developments. Niko recommended the opposite attitude as the only realistic approach to a situation without precedent in history. In all previous generations man had had to come to terms with the prospect of his death as an individual; the present generation was the first to face the prospect of the death of the species. *Homo sapiens* had arrived on the stage about a hundred thousand years ago—which was but the blinking of an eye on the evolutionary time scale. If he were to vanish now, his rise and fall would have been a brief episode, unsung and unlamented. Other planets in the vastness of space were no doubt humming with life; that brief episode would never come to their notice . . .

"Mr. Chairman," Halder interrupted in a mock-distressed voice, "what is this—a summary or a requiem?"

"It's a summary," Niko said dryly, "leading to my last point: the remedies we are meant to propose. If we presume to call ourselves men of science, we must work up the courage to propose the radical remedies which might give humanity a chance of survival. We cannot wait for another hundred thousand years, hoping for a favorable mutation to remedy our ills. We must engineer that mutation ourselves, by biological methods which are already within our reach—or soon will be . . ."

"What do you mean by 'biological methods'?" shouted Halder. "Valenti's needles? Librium in the tap water? Tampering with the chromosomes?"

Solovief gave him a cold stare. His shaggy brows seemed to bristle. "Not exactly that, but something on those lines. I am aware that it sounds frightening, but we should be even more frightened of doing nothing and letting predictable events take their course."

Blood asked in an unusually quiet voice: "Would you put anti-fertility agents into the water supply of the Indians?"

Solovief made a visible effort to break down some inner resistance before he answered. "I would."

"I am with you there," snapped Burch.

John D. John seconded: "So am I."

The others were silent. Claire was reminded of that old soldier's quip: "With my enemies I can cope, but God preserve me from my allies."

Blood said, reverting to his usual manner, "It's all right with *me*. I hate brats anyway."

Wyndham turned to Niko. He did not giggle or titter; even the dimples seemed to have vanished: "Do you suggest including this in the recommendations of the conference? In that case, I am sorry to say, you would have to count me out."

"I do," Niko said slowly, "with some essential qualifications. All governments should be invited to make a last, all-out effort to stop the explosion by appeals to voluntary birth control. If the appeals fail—as they have before and no doubt will again—they should be asked to impose nonvoluntary controls to prevent the catastrophe. I mean *all* nations, regardless of their birth rate, as a gesture of solidarity. Experts should be appointed to work out a plan for moratoriums on birth, for fixed periods at fixed intervals, until the explosion is brought under control. After that, one could revert to voluntary control for a trial period, perhaps with better results."

"Or the opposite," said Harriet. "After the moratorium, everybody will be mad for babies."

"Could be. In that case, the periods of enforced infertility —call them Lent years—would have to be imposed as a more or less permanent feature of human existence—a sort of social calendar to complement the biological calendar imposed by nature."

"And the unborn millions will be grateful to us for being spared death by starvation," said Blood; it was impossible to decide whether he meant it ironically or in earnest.

"I don't know about that," said Niko. "But has any expert, aware of the situation, proposed an alternative?"

"No!" shouted Halder. "And you know why? Because anthropologists and sociologists have respect for human rights and human freedom. You are a physicist, accustomed to smashing atoms."

Niko shrugged. He thought that Otto von Halder as a champion of freedom was a good illustration of what Valenti called schizophysiology. But Valenti himself had been oddly silent during the discussion. Then a possible reason for this occurred to Niko, and he smiled: it was an even better illustration . . .

He squared his shoulders and proceeded to the next point in his notes, which he knew would be even more difficult to put across. Already on the less dangerous subject of imposed fertility control his old friend Wyndham had ratted on him, and Harriet had been unusually noncommittal. Now he had to handle real dynamite: the problem of imposing aggressivity controls . . . He had no hope of persuading them; but he had to go through with it. He took up the thread where Valenti had left off with his remarks about biochemical controls. It was not a problem to be left to the future, because such means of control were already in existence.

"The accumulation of knowledge cannot be stopped, and as man's understanding of his brain increases, new techniques of controlling its functions will be developed at an accelerating pace. The question is no longer whether we like it or not, but how to make the best use of this development with its unlimited possibilities. Nerve gases and hallucinogenic agents to induce mass psychosis are already in existence. Yet any suggestion of putting this new alchemy to benevolent uses is received with horrified outcries and accusations of tampering with human nature. The same outcry greeted Jenner when he introduced vaccination against smallpox—"

"By all means tamper with bacilli, but not with this—not with this!" grunted Blood, hammering his skull with his fist.

Niko copied his gesture. "But *this* is precisely where our troubles reside. This is where evolution slipped up."

"And *this,*" said Valenti, who had regained his smiling composure, pointing at the region of the thyroid gland in his neck, "is where the tendency to cretinism and goiter resides. So the authorities fortify your table salt with iodine without asking your permission."

"I maintain," said Wyndham, "that these are false analogies. Curing or preventing disease is one thing, interference with the mind—if Burch will pardon my expression—is quite another."

"But what if the disease is endemic in the mind of the species? I thought that was our point of departure." Solovief abruptly squashed his cigar in the ashtray. "May I remind you that this is not a discussion of an abstract, academic subject—read today's newspaper headlines, for God's sake." He was almost shouting.

"Emotionalism won't get us anywhere," Halder remarked with judicious glee.

"Rot," said Harriet. "What Niko and Valenti are saying is that emotionalism is all to the good so long as it is in harmony with reason. But they say that there is a fault in the circuitry *here*"—tapping one's skull seemed to have become infectious—"which puts emotion at loggerheads with reason—"

"So you will put some hormones or enzymes into the

tap water and we shall all become like lambs—castrated lambs . . ."

"Contrariwise," remarked Blood, "we might become centaurs—creatures in which the wisdom of a Greek sage is married to a steed's passion."

The vision of Blood transformed into a stallion made Niko relax. "It seems," he said, "that Halder's emotional references to the tap water are a modern version of the archetypal well-poisoning scare. Valenti reminded us that we would have succumbed to epidemics long ago if we had not put chlorine and other stuffs into it. At the same time, we have most effectively polluted our rivers and lakes with mercury, sulphur, cadmium, DDT, and other poisons. But mention the possibility of adding a benevolent ingredient to the list—not a tranquilizer, but a mental stabilizer—and you are all up in arms—"

"Would you consult the population before engaging in a gamble of this kind?" asked Wyndham in an unusually sharp voice.

"Do we consult them before declaring war? Or before suing for peace? Do we consult children before giving them vitamin pills?"

Wyndham shook his head without replying. He was saddened by Niko's frivolity—or the depth of his despair. Or both.

Blood was enjoying himself. "I see that we are in for a sermon on democracy. Pray let me remind you that in 1932 the nation of Hölderlin and Rilke voted, by perfectly democratic means, Adolf Hitler into power. Democracy is too serious a matter to be left to the electorate."

Burch was impressed. "Who said that?" he inquired.

"I say it," trumpeted Blood. "However, I am willing to grant you that it's the lesser evil compared with other alternatives. So long as you don't make a fetish of it."

"Anyway," Niko went on impatiently, "you are skipping

several stages. Nobody suggests that we should start tomorrow adding mental stabilizers to the salt—or the water—though I do believe it will come to that, whether we recommend it or not. The first stage has to be experimenting on a large number of volunteers. Last night Valenti told me of a pilot project he had in mind. Perhaps he will explain . . ."

Valenti got up, adjusting his bow tie. "It is quite simple, my dear colleagues. You collect a thousand volunteers. You pay them. You do not tell them what the experiment is about. You tell them the pills are for having nice dreams while you sleep. During the treatment you arrange for various incidents to occur. The office boss is unpleasant to the subject. He is pushed in the subway by an *agent provocateur.* His wife starts flirting with his best friend. A varied menu of situations designed to provoke aggression and violence. Also one or two *femmes fatales* to invite infatuation, and a prayer meeting in the ashram of a California guru. If the subjects pass all these tests with stoic fortitude, the product can be put on the market. When its effects are shown on television, the use of the product will spread very quickly. It will also spread across the Iron Curtain and the Chinese Wall. Then the tampering, as you say, can be done with public approval. Otherwise it will have to be done anyway."

"Are you talking seriously?" asked Harriet.

Valenti directed the full radiance of his smile at her. "Perhaps it does not sound so, but it is the traditional way of testing a new treatment—the so-called double-blind method. There are controls who are given dummy pills. Neither doctor nor subject knows who gets what."

Suddenly Petitjacques, who had followed the proceedings in silence, with at most a contemptuous grin, spoke up. "This idea I like very much. It is *surrealiste,* it is absurd, and therefore it is good."

"As you realize," said Niko, "Valenti gave us a deliberate parody of his project, perhaps because he realized that to speak seriously would have meant wasting his breath. For once I agree with Petitjacques: the surrealistic world which we have created cries out for surrealistic remedies. Man, biologically speaking, is an artifact, only capable of existing in an artificial environment. I think our only choice is to make it even more artificial in a positive sense. To survive as a species we shall have to change the chemistry—the whole metabolism of the planet's biosphere. Nothing short of that will do. Sermons won't help."

"No, no," Halder shouted. "What we need are more sermons, but not about pincushions and alchemy and changing the metabolism of Faustus' *Erdgeist.* Sermons about peace, more education, more abreaction, more cooperation. It is a pity Kaletski has left us in the lurch. What about that message now? Kaletski should have drafted it . . ."

Halder obviously was so incensed about the rejection of his Therapy by Hate that he even forgot his loathing for Bruno. He lifted his arms in a routine prophetic gesture. "If only, if only, peoples would listen to the voice of reason . . ."

"The point is, they won't," snapped Niko. "If they did, we wouldn't be here, wasting our time talking in circles. I am fed up with this 'if only' philosophy. 'If only' the lion would lie down with the lamb, all would be well. There is an old Russian saying: 'If my grandmother had four wheels she would be an omnibus . . .' "

"Mr. Chairman," said Halder, vibrant with emotion, "I move that you finish your summing up and we then proceed to discuss the Resolution, or message, that is expected from us."

Niko made an effort to pull himself together. Where had he gone off the rails? When he had let himself be carried away by the idea of "biological tampering." *If* there was a road to survival, it pointed in that direction. But did he really believe in that "if"? The familiar, nagging pain had returned. He made a gesture as if brushing a cobweb from his face.

"I must apologize," he continued in a calmer voice, "if I have laid too much emphasis on one, still-hypothetical way out of the impasse into which mankind has maneuvered itself. Other remedies have been suggested by other speakers, which are still vivid in our memories, so I shall not tire you by recapitulating them. With some of these suggestions, such as Halder's and Burch's, I am unable to agree, while with others, such as Wyndham's and Tony's, I am in full sympathy. But they are long-term remedies, and historical time is a tricky dimension—it does not flow at uniform speed, it is accelerating like a river approaching a cataract. It took two thousand years until the dream of Icarus was realized by the Wright brothers' first aerial hop, but only sixty-five years from there to the moon. If the danger to our species is as urgent as in our more lucid moments we know it to be, but in our more relaxed moments tend to forget—then we must have the courage—and the imagination—to seek solutions on a planet-wide scale . . ."

He seemed to have finished, paused, then went on briskly. "In conclusion, may I remind you of that famous Einstein letter that I mentioned in my opening remarks—and which was meant to serve as an inspiration for this conference." The dreaded moment had come. "And so I invite you to make your suggestions regarding the proposed message."

He leaned back in his chair. He had done what he could. In the ensuing silence, the church bells started booming once more, with heavy irony it seemed. The sky over the mountains was an impeccable blue, the glaciers looked more inhuman than ever.

At last Harriet spoke up. "Mr. Chairman, I move that we send no message."

Burch rasped, "Mr. Chairman, I move that we appoint an editorial committee which will prepare a concise and impartial summary of the various proposals that have been discussed, and request a substantial allocation of research funds."

"Burch is right," said Blood. "Asking for funds proves your respectability."

"Mr. Chairman," said Halder, "I move that we all stop making bad jokes."

"Mr. Chairman," said John D. Junior, "I second Professor Burch's proposal."

Petitjacques repeated his dumb show with the Scotch tape. Niko almost sympathized with him. There was another pause; then the swing door opened and Gustav made one of his dramatic entries, saluting in semimilitary fashion, and handing a telegram to the Chairman.

Wyndham giggled: "Hermes, messenger of the gods."

"Reply paid one thousand words," Gustav declared solemnly, and stalked out.

Niko glanced through the text and his face creased into a grimace of disbelief. "Reply paid a thousand words," he repeated. "Hermes got it right. And what perfect timing. It is from Bruno: his proposed draft for our message. Here we go . . ."

He started reading it out, " 'Mr. President . . .' "

Petitjacques shot up, stood to attention, and sat down again, Scotch-taped from nose to chin.

" 'Mr. President, in this crucial hour when the powerful armies of your country are preparing for action to defend the freedom of your people and indeed of the whole planet, we, representatives of diverse branches of the sciences and arts, wish to assure you and your government of our unanimous and unqualified support . . .' It goes on and on, but that's the gist of it."

"Mr. Chairman," Burch said solemnly, "I move that the draft be adopted."

"I second that," said John D. Junior.

Petitjacques tore the Scotch tape off and said fervently, *"Merde."*

Niko's feeling of unreality increased. He inadvertently fell into French: *"Mais ce n'est pas sérieux . . ."*

"Mr. Chairman, I veto the draft," said Harriet. "It is a political statement, and as such outside the terms of reference of this conference."

There were loud murmurs of consent. "I agree," Niko said curtly. "The draft is off the agenda. Where does that leave us?"

With the exception of Burch and John D. Junior, the Call Girls felt so relieved not to have to take a political stand that they hardly realized the full implication of Bruno's message. The atmosphere improved.

Wyndham raised a pudgy hand—it had often been raised, with soothing effect, at similarly critical moments in the history of Oxbridge diplomacy. "It seems, Mr. Chairman, that we have two proposals before us: Dr. Epsom's 'No message,' and Professor Burch's Editorial Committee. But you need at least three people to make a committee, and I doubt whether any three of us would be able to agree on the desirability of the various proposals that have been made, or on the priorities to be assigned to them. If you feel the same way, then the only alternative seems to be: No message. Yet our message, for what it is worth, is already in existence—I mean in the recorded proceedings of the conference. Mr. Chairman, I move that this record be published without delay, and the resulting volume be regarded as the only authentic message emanating from this conference, which will enable the interested reader to make his own choice among the various Approaches to Survival offered to him . . ."

There was a general sigh of relief. Wyndham's proposal was adopted without further discussion. That was the end of the Einstein letter; Wyndham's experienced diplomacy had killed it painlessly. Niko avoided looking at Claire; he felt too numbed to experience regret. He had always known that the conference was a hare-brained idea, and that the famous letter would never materialize. How silly to have talked to Claire about conspiratorial midnight sessions, like a schoolboy. It did not matter. *C'est pas sérieux . . .*

It was nearly six o'clock, and the magnetic field of the cocktail room next door began to exert its influence. Niko still had a few technical announcements to make about honorarium checks and travel arrangements. Tomorrow there would be a special bus leaving for the valley at 11 A.M. Before that, there would be a special mass said in the village church—if anybody happened to be interested. Then he brought the symposium unceremoniously to a close.

It was a night of private post-mortems.

Otto von Halder had invited Hansie and Mitzie to a glass of beer at the Hotel Post. He had tried to get Hansie—the creamy blonde—alone, but she would only go if Mitzie came too. Halder was in an expansive mood, full of *Lebensfreude.* Bruno's resolution had been defeated, Valenti had made a fool of himself, and Niko was a sick, aging man. During dinner at the Kongress cafeteria the radio had been full on, so that all could listen to the news. The contradictory reports about the Asian conflict and the chances of its escalation filled him with the familiar, guilty excitement. But why feel guilty? It was a natural abreaction, and after all, the situation was not of his doing. He entertained the two maidens with the kind of risqué stories which had been so popular in his student years. Hansie giggled dutifully, while Mitzie, the brunette, kept looking sullen. Both had an astonishing capacity for beer. When they absented themselves to the ladies' toilet—together, as was fitting—Halder briefly fell asleep, then rather gruffly asked for the bill and staggered home behind the two girls, who walked, arm in arm, three steps ahead of him, gleefully preparing their detailed account of the evening for Gustav. They were both devoted to Gustav, who had skimmed the cream off both of them several years ago.

Horace Wyndham and Hector Burch were again the last ones at the bar, getting sloshed—Burch in the brisk and purposeful frontiersman manner, Horace according to the principle that the slower you go the farther you get. They were discussing the war in a desultory fashion, Burch taking a patriotic, Wyndham a philosophical line, on the tacit understanding that whatever happened, the groves of academe at Harvard and Oxford would never be defoliated. After the third highball Burch abruptly reverted to his obsession—little Jenny's collection of plaster casts. "You a pediatrician," he mused, "I guess it's only natural . . ."

But Wyndham was unable to give him moral support. His conscience troubled him about Niko. He wondered whether Niko was, after all, right with his brutal proposals for tampering with the biosphere—as if it hadn't already been tampered with! But his instinct and upbringing recoiled from the idea of putting his signature under such a wild document. And what difference would it make anyway?

Harriet Epsom was sitting in front of her dressing table, taking off her make-up with the thoroughness of a picture restorer cleaning an antique landscape. She too was plagued by guilty feelings towards Niko. She was, in fact, half convinced by his arguments—but then why had she kept her big mouth shut? Perhaps because his proposals sounded altogether too Orwellian to her liberal, humanist mind. But if there was really no other way? To hell with the liberal, humanist mind—look where it has got us . . .

There was a knock at the door and Helen Porter walked,

or rather floated in, in a cloud of scent. She wore semi-see-through purple pajamas and her neck was freshly shaven. She made straight for Harriet's bed and covered herself with the voluptuous eiderdown.

"At last," said Harriet, calmly completing her restoration work. "Couldn't you think of it earlier?"

"And what about your gamekeeper with the waxed mustache?"

"That was a mistake," Harriet admitted bravely. "He hurried as if he had to catch a train. Before you could say Jack Robinson it was all over."

Raymond Petitjacques lay neatly tucked up in his bed, indulging in his secret vices: he was munching a chocolate pralinée, of which a whole box stood on his bedside table, and reading Alexandre Dumas' *The Three Musketeers.*

John D. John, Jr., having completed his twenty press-ups on the bedroom floor, was computing a mental balance sheet of Valenti's experiments. He had been particularly impressed by the effects of electrodes implanted in the pleasure centers of the hypothalamus and by the possibilities it opened for erotic self-stimulation, for sex without tears. On the one hand, of course, it deprived the act of the element of interpersonal interrelationship which was supposed to provide part of its enjoyment. On the other hand, these interpersonal interrelationships were the source of untold complications and neurotic entanglements which interfered with one's work. Moreover, the electrodes would enable couples who insisted on such relationships to stimulate each other by radio from distant places without sharing a bed. The method also opened unlimited possibilities for adulterous stimulations. John had a vision of Claire with electrodes implanted under her chestnut hair, and went happily to sleep with it.

Dr. Valenti had recovered his peace of mind. He installed his portable *prie-dieu,* hung the antique silver crucifix over the bed and said his evening prayers. He remembered the fleeting smile on Niko's face during the birth-control discussion: Niko had understood. So what? Sir John Eccles, Nobel Prize for Physiology and Medicine, was a Catholic too.

He felt slightly guilty about having described the experiment with the mental stabilizer in such mocking tones. But he had been provoked almost beyond endurance. And he did not feel justified in telling them that the experiment was actually on its way. Soon after his return the team would have received and tabulated the first results. Then we shall see . . . However, one must beware of the sin of intellectual pride. He was pining to go to confession. Father Vittorio loved to hear about the electrodes, and hoped to have one day Jesus needles implanted in all his flock. Everybody seemed to have needles on the brain nowadays . . .

Tony was unable to go to sleep. The soothing alpha waves failed to make their appearance. He had so much looked forward to this symposium and was bitterly, childishly disappointed. He had no right to judge—but what a vanity fair. And the most painful disappointment had been Solovief himself, on whom Tony had set such high hopes. His arguments had been lucid and logical, but somehow they had failed to convince Tony. Perhaps Niko had even failed to convince himself. Perhaps the reverberations of that archaic lower brain were too strong for the thin voice from the roof to prevail.

He longed to be back at his order's retreat high up in the Atlas—that cool mountain in a hot country—and watching Brother Jonas gently making the roulette ball stop at the preassigned number—playing a game with Newton's laws. To what purpose? To what purpose did that cameo-cutter in

Pompeii, of whom Blood had talked during dinner, go on busily carving his little figure while the lava approached and the ashes engulfed him?

Sir Evelyn Blood, his elephantine bulk propped up in bed, a Victorian nightcap on his balding head, was leafing through a glossy magazine with photographs of athletic-looking male nudes, and at the same time trying to compose a poem. He had two vague images floating in his mind, which he tried to juxtapose in a kind of verbal collage. The first was that cameo-cutter who carried on with a job for which there would never be a buyer. And yet, lo, the cameo was preserved, of priceless value now, and so was its mummified maker, dug out from under the ashes. The second image was a topical version of Balthazar's feast. During dinner at the Kongress cafeteria there had been a moment when they had all frozen, listening to a news announcement on the radio—staring at the loudspeaker on the wall spelling out its *mene tekel.* Then the two images fused into a comic cartoon: the loudspeaker burst open, spewing fire and brimstone, burying alive the whole damned assembly of Call Girls. But it was a cartoon, not a poem.

No good. He composed a haiku instead:

After the thunderclap
the raindrops chatter
discussing the event.

Writing haikus was relaxing, like doing crossword puzzles. He would send it to one of the weeklies, pretending it was a translation from a sixteenth-century Zen master. Twenty quid.

The Soloviefs were sitting on the balcony of their room, silver-plated by moonlight. Niko was explaining the laws of reflection and refraction, as illustrated by looking at the moon through the cylindrical lens of a glass filled with Scotch and water, while Claire was more interested in the color effects. They were not discussing the symposium, nor the boy in the paddyfield, nor Niko's nagging pains. They were waiting for Hoffman, the Director in Charge of Programs at the Academy. He had sat through the sessions unobtrusively in the row of chairs without armrests along the wall. He was still busy settling some administrative matters with the staff, but he had asked whether he might join the Soloviefs for an "informal" drink when he had finished.

"I love the way Americans use the word 'informal,'" said Niko. "They ask you to an informal dinner and it turns out to be a banquet for fifty with three after-dinner speakers. Soon the Justice Department will send out invitations to watch an informal execution in the electric chair."

"Or an informal sex orgy," said Claire.

"I can hardly face him."

"He is a nice, harmless sort of guy."

"And I have let him down."

"They have."

"I have, they have, we have, you have. The fault, dear Brutus, is not in our stars, but in the limits of our imagination. When I have a hangover, I cannot recall the joys of getting drunk. When I am drunk, I cannot evoke the feel of tomorrow's hangover. Honestly, Claire, when you have stuffed yourself with *Knödls,* can you conjure up, by any effort of your proud imagination, the sensation of being hungry?"

Claire shuddered. "Don't talk *Knödls* to me."

"The same impotence of our imagination makes us incapable of believing in tomorrow's apocalypse, even though we can hear the black horses stamping their hoofs. When the 1939 war started, everybody was given a gas mask, but people used the containers as luncheon baskets and left the mask at home. And everybody had to put up blackout curtains, but it was just a game. The law of inertia applies also to the imagination—we cannot believe that tomorrow will be different from today. In this respect sages are no better off than fools. As our symposium so brilliantly demonstrated . . ."

"I am glad," Claire said, "that you do not blame yourself alone."

"But it was my responsibility."

"Anybody else would also have failed."

Their desultory dialogue was put to an end by a loud knock at their bedroom door. A moment later Hoffman's lanky, well-groomed figure appeared on the balcony, reminding Claire of several interchangeable past *beaux* from the Ivy League. "Hello there," he greeted them, sinking into a deck chair, and accepting a glass. "I don't mean to keep you up. But I have something to say to you, Niko, and I don't mind if Claire listens in."

"Fire ahead," Niko said wearily. He had already decided that whatever was going to be said, he would put up no defense.

"I want to say to you, my dear Nikolai, that in the course of my duties I have had the privilege of listening to a considerable number of interdisciplinary congresses and conferences; but never before have I had the good fortune to listen to deliberations more brilliant, stimulating and pertinent to our times than during your symposium. It was great, simply great, to have a confrontation between people like Brother Caspari and Professor Burch—"

"Was there a confrontation?"

"Of course there was. I am sure that when the proceedings appear in print, they will have the same stirring effect which they had on me as an honest Joe and simple administrator. In the name of the Academy I wish to express to you our gratitude and sincere admiration . . ." He solemnly took a measured sip from his glass.

There was a short, uncomfortable, or perhaps informal silence. Claire said, "That was nice, Jerry."

Niko said, "Did you rehearse it?"

"You are incurable," said Hoffman, and did not understand why Claire flinched. "Always frivolous. One wouldn't believe you take things seriously."

"I am an incurable playboy," said Niko. "But now, if you'll excuse me I'll go to bed. It was a memorable day."

But the memorable day had not yet come to an end. Shortly before midnight there was a commotion in the Kongresshaus. Gustav, who slept in the basement, alert even in his sleep, was woken by a confused racket in the Conference Room, and the smell of some acrid, particularly nasty fumes. Donning his army greatcoat, which made an impressive dressing-gown, he rushed to the Conference Room, where a dismal sight awaited him. The large stack of tape recordings, neatly piled up by Claire, was a mass of flames which were just on the point of catching the curtains. On her lonely chair in the corner Miss Carey was watching the display with a saintly smile. There was a thin trickle of blood coming from under her bun, and there were some tiny bits and pieces of electronic equipment and dental cement in her lap. Next to her stood several cans containing some liquid. Meeting Gustav's glance, she explained sweetly, as if talking to a child, that she had not been sure whether the tapes were inflammable, so she had had to douse them with paraffin.

"We call it *petroleum,*" Gustav said severely, busily tearing down the curtains before they went up in flames.

"No, petrol is what we put in motorcars," Miss Carey explained patiently. "It is explosive—that would never have done."

Fortunately Gustav was able to summon two members of the fire brigade from Mitzie's and Hansie's bedrooms. They quickly and competently dealt with the emergency, but the taped proceedings of the Symposium "Approaches to Survival" had been transformed into black cinder.

Saturday

The Soloviefs had decided to stay on for another day and walk in the mountains now that the tourists had gone.

The others were leaving on the bus at 11 A.M. Gustav would take them to the railway station in the valley, from where a train would take them to the airport. Harriet and von Halder were due at a symposium on "Man and His Environment" in Sydney, Australia; Petitjacques was due at a group-encounter live-in at Big Sur, Calif.; Valenti had to attend a neurological congress in Rio de Janeiro, and Blood a P.E.N. Congress in Bucharest. They would pay his return air fare from London which, added to his return fare to Schneedorf, left him with a profit of some fifty pounds.

In view of the international situation, however, nobody could be sure whether they would reach their destination. This added a certain nervousness to the melancholia which always befell the Call Girls at the moment of departure. However much they got on one another's nerves, each symposium grew into a kind of club or family, with its daily routines, its gossip and private jokes. Now it was all coming to an end, and each was again on his or her own. They would not have minded going on for another week.

There were only about ten minutes left. The yellow bus was waiting at the steps of the Kongress terrace. The Soloviefs were sitting on their balcony, watching the loading of the luggage. Soon Niko would have to go down to do the farewell honors.

"I have been thinking," said Niko.

"You have?"

"I thought of a riddle. Tell me the only effective consolation which could be offered a man who knows that he is going to be hanged tomorrow morning at nine o'clock sharp."

"You tell me."

"The prison governor enters the condemned man's cell and says to him: 'We are very sorry, but we have to advance the time set for your execution by thirty minutes. We have just been informed that at nine o'clock the earth will collide with a comet and explode.' "

"Not a very nice riddle."

"But true . . ." He hesitated, then said very gently, "I wanted you to know that I no longer care."

Gustav got into the driver's seat of the bus and honked three times. He was considering whether to get deliberately stuck in one of the spiky virgins to give his passengers a last thrill.

Claire lightly brushed the back of Niko's hand. "You must go down."

"To thank them for their valuable contributions–informally."

Niko clattered down the stairs and took up his position at the plate-glass entrance door–from where he had emerged at the arrival of the bus six days earlier to welcome them on board. Was it only six days? Time enough for the Lord to create a cosmos out of chaos, time enough for man to reverse the process by pressing a few buttons and throwing a few switches. Had it started already? He could not care less.

They were filing out, one by one, cluttered with overnight bags, cameras and attaché cases. A tape-recorder cassette was bulging out of Halder's pocket: it contained his lecture, which he had dug out of the ashes—the only one that had miraculously escaped the flames.

They shook hands with Niko each in turn, putting their baggage on the cement floor while the ceremony lasted.

Harriet kissed him with great aplomb on both cheeks.

"Judas pecked at only one," said Niko.

"Rot," said Harriet, and to his embarrassment, shed some outsized tears.

Halder tried his vicelike grip which left most people's hands numb for a few minutes, but he had forgotten that Niko had spent years exercising on the piano.

Wyndham tittered; Tony blushed; Petitjacques put his index finger across his lips—perhaps indicating that words were meaningless; Niko began to see his point. Blood, looking at him with bloodshot eyes, said with unexpected mildness: "It was not quite such a bad circus as you think."

Dr. Valenti eased Miss Carey through the door with a hand under her elbow, but it looked more like a gallant gesture than one of support, for Miss Carey seemed to have recovered her former serenity, and the gray bun on her head looked as tidy as ever; the doctor probably carried a repair kit, including dental cement, in his elegant leather briefcase.

Burch and John D. John, Jr., walked past in earnest discussion, hardly stopping to shake hands in a perfunctory way. They came last, with the modesty becoming to the victors.

As Harriet and Wyndham were getting into the bus, they

both turned to wave farewell to the massive figure in the rumpled dark suit standing, alone, at the Kongresshaus door.

"He looks ill," said Wyndham.

"He looks like the captain of a sinking ship," said Harriet, "determined to go down with it."

ABOUT THE AUTHOR

ARTHUR KOESTLER was born in 1905 in Budapest. Though he studied science and psychology in Vienna, at the age of twenty he became a foreign correspondent and worked for various European newspapers in the Middle East, Paris, Berlin, Russia and Spain. During the Spanish Civil War, which he covered from the Republican side, he was captured and imprisoned for several months by the Nationalists, but was exchanged after international protest. In 1939–40 he was interned in a French detention camp. After his release, due to British government intervention, he joined the French Foreign Legion, subsequently escaped to England and joined the British Army.

Like many other intellectuals in the thirties, Koestler saw in the Soviet experiment the only hope and alternative to fascism. He became a member of the Communist Party in 1931, but left it in disillusionment during the Moscow purges in 1938. His earlier books were mainly concerned with these experiences, either in autobiographical form, or in essays or political novels. Among the latter, *Darkness at Noon* has been translated into thirty-three languages.

After World War II, Mr. Koestler became a British citizen, and all his books since 1940 have been written in English. He now lives in London, but he frequently lectures at American universities, and was a fellow at the Center for Advanced Study in the Behavioral Sciences at Stanford in 1964–65.

In 1968 Mr. Koestler received the Sonning Prize at the University of Copenhagen for his contributions to European culture, and in 1972 was made a Commander of the British Empire. His works are now being republished in a collected edition of twenty volumes.